erret

★

C·P·SERRET

AMERICAN FICTIONS

TEMPEST & GAYLE,
PHŒNIX,
MMXXV.

Published by
Tempest & Gayle
PHOENIX

American Fictions is a work of fiction. Names, characters, places, and incidents either are the products of the author's imagination or are used fictitiously. Any resemblance to actual persons, living or dead, businesses, companies, events, or locales is entirely coincidental. No part of this book may be used or reproduced in any manner for the purpose of training artificial intelligence technologies or systems.

Design by C. P. Serret

Paperback cover art George Frederic Watts

Set in Seria

ISBN: 979-8-9926708-6-8

AMERICAN FICTIONS

NEVER HUMAN

Tu ſe ombra, et ombra uedi.
—DANTE, Purgatorio, Canto XXI.

★

C·P·SERRET/ NEVER HUMAN/ I.

He learned to swallow his voice. Hollow things echo. Don't speak.

—*That*, she said.

She was pasty and soft, pointing with a limp, withdrawn hand. Green eyes. No, greenish grey, not looking at him.

Sideways in her seat, her limp hair was dead yellow grass crowned with a rainbow of butterfly clips. There was no mistaking it. The pinched eyebrows, the crinkled nose, and the twisted upper lip of her open mouth.

He was encircled by her clique, caught in his cold blue chair, a shiny woodlike tablet angled above his legs. They were all like that. Columns and rows. Everyone caught.

The room was grey, but it was green and open outside the glass. Grey like the City Of, but that was far away. It smelled green outside, but not in here.

He hadn't listened to what they'd been saying, their awkward lines, like when the TV is on and you aren't watching. They each would say things, and the others would echo them. Or pretended to. Or were supposed to.

—Ismaël, the French Madame called him, est-ce que vous parlez anglais?

—Sí...

The chorus groaned, but Madame talked about the French si in English; then she called on someone else. It was all rote. Like a basic echo command:

French Mme:~> echo «Je parle français!»
Je parle français!

The French Madame was American and taller than the tallest boy in the grey room and had big yellow hair like a star in an old movie. With her squeaking white cursor, she scrawled on the green plane that covered most of the front wall. Command lines.

Dead Grass had turned back around in her seat. Her layered tank bared her shoulders and upper back, giving him a glimpse of the razor edge of her hollow. Her softness was as thin as an eggshell, the visible sliver of emptiness in unlit shadow.

They were all the same under their tees, polos, and button-ups. All hollow.

It was hard not to look, impossible not to see it wink when she squirmed in her seat. No one, not even the smaller ones at the red house, had ever admitted to seeing it, but they knew how to lie, too. He'd learned to play off the «joke»; then he'd stopped joking.

You could feel the invisible surface, the warm skin over sinew and bone. Like a glass egg with a partially painted shell, you can see inside, but you can't stick your finger in. A surface that showed in mirrors, photos, and on TV, through windowpanes or an empty glass. Even Saran Wrap.

His own back, in the mirror, too, showed unbroken skin. There was no way to see, no way to be sure. He only saw hollows directly with his naked eyes.

Most of the time, he didn't think about it. Most of the time, he didn't have to see. But it was hard not to look at that beckoning gap into shadows till one of the others teased, hissing,

—Omigod, he's staring: I think he likes you.

There were muted *ewws* and other mimes of outrage till Madame called on one of them. He listened to everyone say what they were supposed to say, stumbling and faltering on cue.

Words were less than empty. He watched every hollow gesture, every feigned expression. Each was alone in her performance, following her cues, as isolated as his observance. The buzzer ended the routine.

They poured out of the grey room into a grey hallway patched with sections of blue. It looked the same in both directions. Rows of doors, sharp turns right and left, stairwells down and up. A square circuit of rooms, three levels high. They bunched and flowed past each other in a fluid dynamic. More lines. Barking. Hooting. Routines and subroutines.

The carpet was cleaner than the sidewalks in the City Of. He sat by himself against the wall like they did together, on standby for the next thing. You started with a sheet of numbers and times. Each number was a room, the times a sequence of rooms. A program of routines. A loop of the program till they give you a new sheet.

His bookbag was a darker grey, like concrete in the rain. He took out his pad and a yellow pencil, No. 2. It wasn't finished. There was pressure behind each line, an incompressible solidity that travelled down through the fragile graphite tip.

Pale-blue doll eyes, clear and shiny like glass, she looks down at him. Long hair, yellow gold, she wears shades of blue. The blue jeans faded. The blue polo, navy; the little man and horse, red. She says, She's such a bitch.

He shrugs, saying, Nothing new. He didn't want to say anything.

You're Ismael, right? I'm Sophie.

Her features are sharp, the only softness implied by the diffusion of light over her skin. She drops and sits cross-legged beside him; she smells like soap. Green soap. You like to draw?

He shrugs.

Sophie says, What are you drawing? A cowboy?

A robot from an old movie.

Why would a robot dress up like a cowboy?

He doesn't know he's a robot.

How can he not know?

Nobody told him.

Is he even a him?

He thinks so.

Can he really think, or is he just pretending to?

Ismael shrugs again and says, How could you tell the difference?

Sophie watches him draw, then says, You like machines?

All the parts have to fit together. I can understand them.

Even when they don't understand themselves? Is that okay?

Ismael doesn't have an answer to that. Is it worse to know?

She says, Don't you think they're scary?

He says, Scarier than what?

The doors opened. The Art Misses was grey, turning white. The art rooms were white, like the inner surface of the hollows. It was like stepping inside.

A place of flat surfaces and solids. He'd asked the Science Mister about curved surfaces without saying *hollow*, and he'd said that was mathematics. He asked the Math Mizz, and she talked about advanced placement.

Waiting clusters dispersed to the level-top desks set edge-to-edge in unbroken white rows. All mid and longer-haired, shes: yellow hair, brown, and red, but for him. His was short and, in mirrors, black. He preferred to sit in the middle, in the gaps between their clusters. He'd learned to hide in the crowd.

A new assignment, Art Misses explained. Mixed media. Not the unambigüous surfaces he preferred but one cluttered and obscured.

No pencils, then, or ink, but acrylics, glue, and aluminum foil. Matte side out, the lid of a trash can was seated ajar, as seen from above. A tilted circle. The inside was only a crescent, shiny side out, a fuzzy mirror in oblonged eclipse. A dollop of putty on the sidewalk grid painted black like old bubblegum. Period. Signed, Icy. He had nothing else to say – he'd been nabbed tagging «Icy» and had ended up in the System.

The Art Misses asked if everything was okay: they had two periods to finish. She suggested an impasto technique to add pavementlike texture. Next time.

Sophie meets him on the stairs, going down. Lunch? she says.

He nods but is still on the trash can: he hasn't thought about them as a shape – another complex surface around a hollow. He'll have to look at one on the way to the red house. There might be more details.

Her green soap is lost in the shuffle of heated breath and stale, mid-day sweat. She says, Is Art your favourite class?

I guess.

Could you draw me? she says, smiling.

I guess, but not for class.

Okay, later.

He split off with some of the shuffling shoes into a wider, dimmer space. Grey pillars rose to the high ceiling. It didn't smell like the lanes outside of restaurants at dinner time. There was the acrid tinge of smoke on steam and a thicker pungence: meaty, metallic, and acid. The feed was twice a day. More than the soup kitchens, but the smell was about the same.

Long lines were nothing new, and compared to back then, he wasn't even hungry. It was spooned out with long satin-silver handles. Covered hair. Smooth steel surfaces, not those crinkle-cornered aluminum trays.

Rows of rectangular brown planes rested on black webs of tubing. Orange ellipses were suspended alongside them. Rigid lines of separation and mushroomlike perches for stranger things than cartoon caterpillars.

They segregated themselves by hair length. He sat, centring himself within an interstice, three empty seats on each side. Shorter-hairs only on this half of the space.

The tray was orange, too. Flat bits of sheet metal, an eggshell plate, three wet blots, yellow, brown, and green.

They complained about their spoonfuls. He'd had worse, but he knew the emptiness folding in towards his spine like a twisted balloon.

No matter how much they ate, they were always empty. You could complain when you weren't hungry or afraid. They'd never had to search or hide except as a game.

—Hey!

Puffy, pasty, too, and piglike.

—Hey, where are you from?

Ruddy surfaces, bowl hair. Not a part of his program either. Ismael said,

—Here?

—Why's this kid so stupid? Where? are? you? from?

They wanted something farther away.

—Belize, said Ismael.

—Where the fuck is that? Mexico?

—Central America.

—So, Mexico. Jeez, this dumbass.

Piggy said,

—Why don't you go back there?

—I can't, said Ismael.

—Why not?

—I was born here.

—So? You can still go back

Ismael shook his head. There was no going back – not from the trash.

—This dumbass...

The other gaps would be the same, and he could see *that* girl from here. April. Long, dark, straight hair. There was something different about her, though she was the same: the same gestures, the same lines. She was in part of his program.

He cleaned his plate, and they started in on him again, mocking how he'd finished his peas off of the tipped surface. Are you gonna cry? they said. Gonna cry?

Quitting the routine, «this dumbass», the «*that*», and sometimes «it», returned his tray. Outside, a blacktop grid of chalk lines painted with broad brush strokes. He'd emerged from the wide rectangular brick surface, a line of «happy trees» opposite. The blacktop was a charcoal rub, uneven shades of grey, the grid, a gameboard of leftover Hot Wheels. There were lots of brick walls in the City Of, lots of grey towers, lots of glass. Lots of Hot Wheels. Every surface was subject to the interplay of shadow and light, even their inner surfaces.

This wall was like one side of a cube sunk into the ground. On the other side was the open green with its fences, but *they* would be there, too. The liquid plane above was marbled blue and white, an upside-down sea.

It was a middle place, they'd said, before a higher place. The higher place would also be a middle place. A «preparatory» place for the last middle place, before «your future». Unless he chose more middle places. You had to choose your programs in advance, and that, too, was a test. That's what they'd said when they'd picked this program for him this time: trilingual better than bilingual. Next time, it was his test. They were a part of the System.

For a long time, he'd been stuck outside. He'd been cold. He'd been wet. He'd looked into grey buildings, brick buildings like this one, empty at night with their lights on. Their clean, dry carpets. He'd slept on the pavement right next to their locked doors. Slept under overhangs that staved off the rain or the morning dew and in hollows that let the wind blow by. You had to lay something down over concrete's leeching cold, but he'd learned to leave before anyone showed up. To make it like he'd never been. Leave no trace and use it again.

He'd bought a Casio with his lawnmower money. Their Swatchs stepped from second to second, showing the hollow between moments. LCDs covered the gaps behind a digital mask. Covered what was hidden in *now*. It was time, now, to go back. There was no buzzer outside, but the shadows had changed shape. Some of them had folding radios that showed the time, but the misters and misses would take them if they saw.

Passing from outside to inside, a membrane of tension tried to repel him. The plastic light, grey walls, and the steps of uncounted sacrifices. For the future. He'd heard the tears of children bring rain, but they didn't know that here or didn't say. *That* was Mexico.

Had he really been Kekchí, too? Had he counted? Sacrificed not to a Well, but thrown to the City Of. He'd lost the names, except for the god of mountains, but there were no mountains near.

Long hairs crowded the front row of the grey space, variations on a theme. Bright shirts, jeans, and shorts. He sat in the second, not behind April, but on the diagonal. Her bare legs were crossed away from him, one bare foot freed of its boat shoe. A contrast of surfaces. Translucent white marble, brown leather – LL Bean, like a lot of them. He was learning.

Her brown hair was centre-parted and curled only against her clothes. It would be hard to paint, streaked with lighter strands. Her eyes, never looking at him… charcoal, Ti white, and a dab of Prussian blue. He could follow the thin arcs of her eyebrows, the uptilt of her nose. The swollen crescents of her lips, smiling not at him. *Flesh tint* acrylic.

He traced the line of her limb, over the knee and down her instep, to the piano-key fit of her small toes. Pressure surged down to its level. It pulsed, an aching discomfort reaching out to her, tight against his thigh.

What trudged in behind her wasn't the Math Mizz but a Substitute Mister, almost grey in his faded dishevelment. Hunched plaid; chinos; and a dilapidated bag, brown leather. A hollow folded in on itself.

—Shoes on, please.

Ismael flinched from the Substitute Mister, noticing him noticing. A bland, lined, grey face, dead eyes, toad eyes. Eyes painted on. A squashed toad mouth that found everything wanting.

April shifted upright in her blue seat, turning. He clenched his pencil, and the throbbing subsided into a sulking disquiet. The Substitute Mister handed out two sign-in sheets and pens at each end of the front row. He took up the white cursor then began to draw: Mr...

A white sheet appeared over Ismael's shoulder with a blue-capped Bic. He drew *Ismael_Canul* in a single calligraphic line without lifting the point. They were looking at each other, muffled giggles, as he handed them forward. Then,

—Eww, it's warm.

She held the pen out. Mocking, feigned grimaces. Conspiring, April said,

—What was he doing with it?

Neither looked at him; he wasn't there. She passed April the paper and the warm pen. Another *eww.*

Ismael wasn't going to cry. He swallowed it down with the wet lumps of yellow, brown, and green. He should've stayed in the middle.

Don't forget that face. Her face. It was only a surface. No one was solid unless he sculpted them with his own hands.

White lines on the black plane, a geometry simpler than what he was looking for, but a building block. Like LEGOs. Like bricks in the wall. Like letters in a word – the language of surfaces.

He looked again. Along the complex curves of April's foot, half in its shoe, the rosy highlights of her sole, it resurged. Biting his underlip, he looked at the white lines on black, an eggshell structure from the side.

Something turned over in his gut. Want. Frustration, a wet, sour lump, but he swallowed it.

He looked past her.

★

C · P · SERRET,
NEVER HUMAN, II.

T*he metal tube stank* of green vinyl, foam, and black rubber. It was a relief to step out into the green air. Yellow and black, warning colours; on black rubber, it trailed black soot.

I'll walk with you, Sophie says.

Curved black strips carved through the green, striped with yellow dashes down their centres. Warning colours. The happy trees were spaced apart like the large boxes separated by wood slats and covered in wood slats. White, red, and blue irregular pentagons. Flag colours. Some flags.

In the City Of, the strips were small and twisted, cracked and divoted. The boxes were taller and pressed closer together, the cars jammed everywhere. Here, each box had its own dead end, perpendicular to the strip. It was quiet. In the City Of, there was always something shrill. Something screaming.

It's like there's no one else here, Sophie says.

But there were cars in their dead ends. Behind the horizontal slats, behind the unshuttered glass, they were there. Or they weren't till you opened the door. There was no way to be sure – there was nothing solid.

It's like ghosts, he says. They're kind of there even when you can't see them.

Creepy. So, if there's, like, five billion of *them* out there, but we can't see them, then the whole wide world is haunted, right? Are we ghosts, too?

How would we know?

Which house is yours?

The small red one.

The red house was a pentagonal prism like most of the wooden boxes. It had the same lawn as the house next door, but he only mowed inside the white slats.

Which room is yours? she asks.

Around the left side, the corner in back.

Wait, she says as he opens the gate, when will you draw me?

Maybe later. I have homework.

The door was never locked. He could hear the screaming before he opened it. The smaller ones couldn't play without screaming. The walls were papered with squiggly lines, and the small ones crayoned across them. Mixed media.

Matchbox cars were scattered over long woodgrain tiles. A metal shell on top and plastic on the bottom, they flexed when you squeezed them. Hollow, too.

Timmy couldn't keep his shirt on, bashing two cars together while droning aloud. The oval edge of the opening in his back was thinner than paper. As thin as light.

The reversed contours of his chest and belly were defined by shadows, the arm holes pitch black without a flashlight. Not peach-cream like his skin, but a seamless titanium-white. Like the shiny paint of a brand-new car with a sticker on the glass.

No one was looking at the flickering cube on one side of the space. A *living* room, where the bulbous cube played out life on one bowed glass side. And there, on that curved surface, Nancy's soaps and *War in Iraq* were solid.

He'd asked the Science Mister about mirrors and lenses, about how they *created* an image. The Science Mister had talked about advanced placement.

Ismael went to his room. There were three small ones, and they weren't allowed inside. They shared a room upstairs near Frank and Nancy. The bigger two had their own rooms, too. There were always six from the System.

On his file, he was a number. They all were, and the red house was a middle place, not a «home» like they called it. A home business. The older ones would have to leave soon; then, he would be next.

It was the same colour as the lunch plates: «Eggshell», Nancy had said to his question. There were images taped up on the walls, «bands», her word. *Pink Floyd*. *Led Zeppelin*. They'd been here when he'd arrived, and he left them up. He was ready to go anytime.

On the small desk, his *Appleseed* books. The rest of his lawnmower money. He had volumes one and two. Three was next year, or shell out for the back issues. A ruined world of computers and machines. Their future. The machines were very detailed, but he had to do his own designs. Not copy.

Ismael sat on the bed. He had take-home tests: Geometry. Social. French. It was part of the routine. Maybe later.

He took the pad and pencil from his bookbag. He sketched two light ovals, intersecting, then shorter oblongs, a row of small circles. Then he began to connect the shapes, a heavier line to define April's foot. To make it solid. The shading would come last, but he stalled on the smaller details. The exact shape of the nails, the contours of her toes… The details were fuzzy, but then, he couldn't remember the colour of her eyes either.

He couldn't use his own foot for reference. It wasn't even close.

His door didn't lock, but they usually didn't barge in. It was still a risk. He slipped off of the bed and reached between the box spring and mattress. He slipped out a crinkled, brown paper bag.

Inside were two glossies. One was *Entertainment for Men* from Jake, the bigger boy. The other was *Fashion* but titled in French. Addressed to Nancy on a white label, he'd lifted it from the mail. The first showed everything; the second, even more.

They were magnetic and repellant, from glossy covers to glossy pages. He'd shuddered the first time, running his fingers over solid torsos, the line of the spine going down. Over the ripples of muscle and bone, but the paper was smooth and cold. The camera adds ten pounds, he'd heard them say. Even they knew there was a difference.

Was it the lens? The interpretative surface that made three dimensions two, making hollow solid? He'd looked for books at the library but hadn't asked the librarian. Nor had he talked to the Science Mister or the Math Mizz about looking at three dimensions from two. They would bring up advanced placement.

The one «for men» didn't show them much. The other, here and there. He found the pose he needed. *That* picture: in the blue dress. Curly dark hair, red smiling lips, her legs bare from the knee down. Not crossed, but at the correct angle, away from him. The first time he'd looked at it – entranced, looking at them, something had spotted his briefs.

He compared the sketch. Of course, April's wasn't the model's. But there were clues, reminders, and inspiration. It responded again, but he focused on the dulling pencil tip, its drag on the white paper. On the manifold of grey lines, till a sharp *wrap! wrap!* on glass.

A small white fist. He flips the pad and hides the glossies. Looking up on the other side of the glass, Sophie. The window lifts with a wood-on-wood groan.

Help me up, Sophie says.

Why are you… ?

You said you'd draw me.

Okay, he says, then helps her up and over the window sill. She says, Where should I sit?

Wherever, he says, shrugging.

You were drawing on your bed? I'll sit in the chair.

Sophie pulls the chair away from the small desk and rotates it toward the narrow bed. She sits and asks, What were you drawing?

Nothing, he says. He flips to a blank page and shifts to the edge of the mattress.

How should I pose?

Take off your shoes. And socks.

Should I take off anything else?

No.

Sophie unlaces her white canvas sneakers, Superga, and unrolls her white socks.

Put them up on the edge of the chair, then spread your fingers on your insteps.

She draws up her legs, then rests her head between her knees. She says, Fingers and toes?

They're the hardest to draw, he says. And noses. Look over there.

She turns her head. A three-quarter profile. He roots in his bag for the pencil sharpener, then flips to a fresh sheet. He starts over.

The light changes, and he hesitates over the shadows. He rubs his fingertip, dented by the pencil. A solid hexagon.

What would it take to make Sophie solid? Not just in clay

or marble, but moving and talking like the «Gunslinger». With pistons, wires, and gears. Like that.

Is it done? Sophie asks.

There was a knock at the door.

—Yes, he said.

It swung open. Nancy said,

—Have you finished your homework?

—Not yet.

She stepped into the room. Her straight, dark bowl-cut hair, her surface leathery and lined. She was taller than him but not by much; she looked at his pad upside down.

—Your drawings are very good, but you do have to finish your homework. Is that a friend from school?

—No; I made her up.

—Come to the kitchen; we need to talk before dinner.

—Okay.

He left it where it was and followed. Two of the three small ones were seated on the floor, watching lines move on the curved glass. Drawings were always solid, even when they moved. Even when they sang «Row row row your boat» and changed the words. High RPM record player voices. *The Chipmunks' Life* is just a dream. Timmy bashed yellow plastic trucks in the corner, a white hole flickering with the bulb.

The kitchen smelled like the school cafeteria. Boiled greens and tomato sauce: a casserole and broccoli. Hamburger Helper.

Frank had a big, lumpy nose, his surface carved with drooping hangdog lines. The kitchen floor was linoleum, a carved grid. In art, they'd carved white linoleum with channel knives. Grooved the surfaces to print on another surface. Frank's buttoned-up shirts were printed with lines like the wallpaper.

—Nancy, close the door. Izzy, we got a call from your school counsellor today. He said your art teacher talked to him about a painting you did for class. He was concerned. Frank nodded as he talked, agreeing with himself:—Look, Izzy, we have a lot of experience working with the System. You have to play along. Tell 'em what they want to hear. You didn't ask to be in the game, but you are, and you're starting with a handicap. Don't tell anybody I said that, but you are ¶.

Right now, the cards are against you. You're behind the curve. They're looking for any reason to sideline you, and you can't give them one. You know what you're supposed to say, what they expect, amirite? I don't have to tell you. When they ask you to draw a family. You know what to do.

Ismael said,

—They threw me away.

They left me to die, he didn't say.

—And if you get stuck on that, Frank said, that's where you'll end up again. The System doesn't forgive. If you say or do anything they don't like, they'll get rid of you ¶. Your file will get lost, your application thrown away. They'll erase you ¶. Everything is part of the System. Everything ¶. You're smarter than the others, and that makes it harder. You want to question things. Play ball instead ¶. When other people clap, you clap. When other people smile, you smile.

—You want me to pretend.

—Every single day. From when you wake up until you go to bed. You have to fool everybody. If somebody asks how you are, you say *good*. Not *fine*.

—No, Nancy said. You're doing *great*.

—Don't do it for us, Frank said, or because we told you to. Do it for you ¶. You're from Belize. You were never homeless. Your parents are *gone*. You have a foster family. That's how you say it ¶. *Family*, not just *parents*.

You had to be precise with the System, like filling in those little ovals on a test. No. 2 only. Keep it inside the lines.

Ismael said okay to everything.

Jake met him in the hallway.

—Hey, 'lil dude. I'm gonna need *that* back.

—Okay, Ismael said.

He didn't mind; he didn't need *that*. He gave *that* back first, then closed his door, then sat on the bed.

Sophie says, Why did they throw you away?

I could see through them.

You're not like them.

You don't know that. There's no way to know.

They know you're different.

These? On the surface. They don't see anything else.

What you do matters. They just warned you. The System.

I can only do what they tell me. Only say what they tell me. It's the same as telling me to disappear.

Maybe it's like that for them. Think about it. They had to choose, too.

«Be an architect; be an engineer». They already chose for me.

You *can* do it, though. That's what they're saying.

They're tying my hands.

You have to take control – tell them you want to be an artist. You can't stay here.

I'll be out there, alone. Again.

He takes a deep breath. A deep sigh.

She says, If things were different, could it have been you and me? Us?

No, he says. You'd be just like them.

A white hole, she whispers. Like that bitch in French.

Like April, he didn't say. And now I have to be like them, too. The surface they want to see. Whether I am or not.

She shakes her head with a sad smile and reddened eyes. Hide, she says. Hide under their noses, but don't be empty. Never be empty. Promise me.

He considers. He can't see it – doesn't know what it means – but he says, If there is a way, I'll find it.

His drawing of her was solid. She wouldn't just disappear.

Ismael picked up the pencil. He had an idea.

★

C·P·SERRET,
NEVER HUMAN, III.

T*hou ſeeſt, we are not all alone vnhappie:*
This wide and vniuerſall Theater
Preſents more wofull then the Sceane
Wherein we play in.

ISMAEL
All the world's a ſtage
And all the men and women meerely Players:
The haue their Exits and their Entrances;
And one man in his time playes many parts,
His Acts being ſeuen ages. At firſt, the Infant,
Mewling, and puking in the Nurſes armes.
Then, the whining Schoole-boy, with his Satchell,
And ſhining morning face, creeping like ſnaile
Vnwillingly to ſchoole.

The chorus laughed. The English Misses asked,
—And what does that mean to you, Ishmael?
—That everything's made up. It's all fake. Everyone is pretending.

The chorus laughed again. The English Misses asked,
—Anyone else? Johnathan.
—That everyone has a place in the world. That we all go through the same stuff.
—Very good. The human condition. You'll hear this...

Ismael knew better, but no one would listen. Except the System, and every answer was a test. Frank and Nancy weren't wrong.

He was in, or he was out. With every 0, he was downgraded. He'd pass through with every 1. April was up front, so he'd moved to the back. Away from her and her 1s. She was still pretty... on the surface. It was like two magnets when turned the other way.

But it was becoming clearer: a sorting program. Habitual 0s sat in the back till they were sorted out and collected into different routines. Put on different tracks.

The Homeroom Misses had told him he wasn't in trouble, but he had to see the Counselling Mister after English. Unlike French or Latin, English wasn't about English. He had to read *Webster's New World Pocket Dictionary* and *The Elements of Style* for himself. Red, white and blue, two old books left behind by whoever had left the posters behind. Or someone before them – someone else from the System.

A noose was snugged up around the Counselling Mister's neck. The flat belt of blue hung down over the buttons of his button-up. The Principals wore nooses, too. And the talking busts on that glass screen. Tight under their collars, nooses ensured their hollows would never show and hid the buttoned seam down their front. Nothing to see here.

The Counselling Mister's hair was neatly parted on one side. His mouth curved a lot, but his eyes didn't change behind his thin, wire-rimmed spectacles.

—Given where you're coming from – and there's no shame in that. But given that, your foster parents asked for extra guidance into what's expected of you ¶. We want you to know that you have many options. It can be more difficult for gifted children to fit in, but we don't want you to feel disadvantaged in any way ¶. You've been recommended for Honours Math. We'd normally wait till next semester, but we're prepared to move you mid-term. You'll have to work hard to catch up, but I'm sure you can do it ¶. And the sooner you are on the AP track, the better. You'll be the first Hispanic student to take AP Trigonometry at West. Do *you* think you're ready?

Track was a word Ismael had already flagged.

—Do I have to decide now?

—No, but the sooner you get onto your track, the better. Some people will tell you that you don't have to decide now, that you can wait for college to find yourself. That might be okay for average students without intellectual curiosity or personal drive. But to reach for the highest track, we should prepare you now ¶. The worst thing we could do is leave you unchallenged. You could become bored, even drop out.

—I get it.

—The sooner you have an idea of what you'd like to accomplish in the future, the sooner we can get you on track to succeed. While most of our students go to West, you can apply to East or even look into a scholarship at a private academy ¶. West has the superior Art program and a good range of AP courses, but East focuses on college prep. It also has a challenging IB diploma program, and you may qualify for exam fee waivers. Is there anything you've thought about?

The Art Misses had talked about West and art schools. He'd listened.

—I've already decided.

The Counselling Mister leaned forward, picking up his pen.

—Excellent! What were you thinking of?

—I'm going to build robots. Like in the movies, but better.

—That's exactly what I like to hear. Something ambitious. Like computers, robotics will be important in the future. You've seen how the automotive industry uses robots to make cars?

—A little. I looked for books on it, but the library doesn't have any.

—Proactive. You have a bright future if we can channel those energies productively. I'll put *Robotics Engineer* as your career goal ¶. There are no guarantees, but you should set your aim high: the major technical schools. MIT. Caltech. Graduate studies, I assume?

—Whatever it takes.

—Are you willing to give up access to the Art program at West?

—Yes. IB at East, you said?

—I'll make some calls. As long as you apply yourself, I think we can make it happen. Your GPA is critical going forward, not just in Honours Math but across the board. You'll need to take every subject seriously and have high participation ¶. Avoid spreading yourself too thin with unneeded electives. Honours English, for example, can wait until you're at East, and then you can decide to keep French or Latin for your IB. You will need one of them ¶. Extracurriculars will become unavoidable once you're there, too. But for now, let's focus on bringing your GPA up to a three-point-nine by the end of next year. Study and homework need to be an everyday habit. Attendance, perfect if possible. Think of a missed day as a handicap on your GPA ¶. What you do today determines your doctorate a dozen years from now and the rest of your future. It's hard when you're eleven or twelve to think about where you'll be in your twenties. But the clearer your goal is to you, the easier it will be to do what's needed every day in order to succeed. «The journey of a thousand miles begins with a single step» – it's an old saying from the Far East. We'll start you in Honours Math next week.

Ismael said okay to everything and took mental notes. It was the machinery of the System. The right routines to get on the right track through the right programs. From middle place to middle place, the steps of a pyramid leading up and up and up. One mistake and you'd get stuck or fall down.

For most, their track kept them on the level they were born into. Most climbers failed, and falling off your track left you on a lower step or back where he'd begun. He'd seen it all from the gutter. Those who'd fallen, those who broke. Those who disappeared.

It was a glimpse into the source code of the sorting program. The acronyms and keywords. *Success*. That's how he would have to talk, too. *Good*, not *okay*, like Frank said.

He walked the deserted circuit, bookbag on one shoulder, blue pass in hand. In a way, it was worse than being out there. Harsher. Colder. There was no place for him, not as himself.

The pass crumpled. With the right surface, he would pass through. He grimaced at a sinking nausea.

He smoothed the pass and handed it to the Science Mister. He sat on the front row next to April. He was still looking ten or twelve years ahead, at how old he'd be then – at what he'd be doing. The middle places looked smaller if you were stepping over them.

The science routine was easy, and he usually input the 1s when it stalled. At the head of the class, there was no need to look to his sides. No need to look back.

He didn't look forward to Gym. To the locker room, to the white holes. He didn't mind swimming, but watching the water swirl around their emptiness… He focused on his stroke, on his breathing. The Gym Mister had talked about the swim team; if not here, then at West.

Maybe at East, if that's what it took. If he had the stomach for it. He didn't have the stomach for lunch and went to the library. It was quiet.

You're not going to eat? Sophie says.

Not hungry.

Are you sure about this?

Lunch? he says.

About giving up art. It's all you have.

I'm not giving up art. I'm going to make machines that *are* art.

It's not the same. You won't be an artist.

I'll be an engineer, like they said.

For me? She spreads her hands in front of him. For this?

What I engineer will be art. You.

I'm afraid. I'm afraid you won't be able to turn back.

I can't. I'm on a track, like a train. As soon as I left that office.

Can you even make something real after you become a liar? After you spend twenty or thirty years as a liar?

Everything I need to know is behind their doors, and they can lock me out. They don't want to see me – they want to see what they want to see – like the school counsellor. They used to try so hard not to see me that they would actually step on me while I was sleeping. They'd stand on me like I wasn't even there. Or like it didn't matter, like I was trash on the sidewalk. If I said anything, they would just look at me with these dead eyes they have and not even move their foot. Like Frank and Nancy said, there's no other way.

And it's making you sick to your stomach.

I'll get used to it.

And then, what kind of monster will you make?

Like in the movies, but better.

It's too late to save you.

I decided yesterday.

Why, she asks, because you had a wet dream?

The spasms had lifted him to consciousness under a puddle, her face a lingering spectre.

That's not the reason

Yes, it is.

Those other kids will join the Army, or work at a supermarket, or go to jail. I've heard all the stories. I won't be like them.

The next program wasn't part of what he would build. But it was part of his track, and he had to «play ball», as Frank said. Play along for a 3.9. If it was a pyramid with four steps, it was too late to reach the peak. Here, but not at East. Not at the middle place after that. There was still a chance. Ismael could still do it.

3.9 came first. He moved through the circuit with purpose. He sat on the front row – at the end, the last at the head of the class, for now.

The Social Mister had hair around his jaw and chin. Most of the misters didn't. He called out a series of names. Alphabetically, by the names he didn't say. Called him *Ishmael*.

—Here.

—Ah, I didn't see you on that side. How're you?

—Good.

The names went on. Ismael could say good and not *okay* and didn't feel anything. He could say it to *Ishmael* and not complain. He could play ball.

Sophie sits on the grey carpet, legs and arms crossed. Red around her eyes. She doesn't say anything. She watches him input 1s, then passes him a note.

He unfolds it: WHAT A BIG NOSE YOU HAVE.

I'm busy, he scrawls on the other side and gives it back.

She pens another line and makes a football fold. She tosses it onto his open history book: IS IT WORSE TO BE HOLLOW OR TURN TO WOOD?

He writes back, Better wood or metal or even mud than hollow.

She writes for a long time on the back of the unfolded sheet, then back on the front. He takes notes and inputs 1s. Participation.

Sophie refolds it back in on itself, inside out. Another lob, then she stalks out. No return address.

The black ink riding blue lines, her bubbly letters were big and small this time:

A boy dreamed of a girl, but she wasn't real.

The boy was real, but the Devil said, I can make you a deal, and one day, boy, you'll be able to make a metal girl. The Devil wore a tie and glasses and had a magic pen, but the Devil said, You can't sign 'cause a boy's soul don't belong to hisself. But Them, Them offered me the boy's soul. Caesar gave them silver, and they polished Caesar's fine silver. And Them told the boy his flesh 'n' blood was bought 'n' sold, but there was one more thing to sell. Sell it, boy, Them tells him, and we'll sign on the dotted line. It's all you gots left. The Devil is waiting.

The boy longed for the dream and told the Devil, Take this no-good soul. And the boy became cold, stiff, and shiny all over. A clockwork boy full of gears and springs. His nose is a yard long but doesn't get bigger 'cause he can only tell lies. And when he moves, it winds his spring, and the wheels go tick tick tick 'cause wooden boys don't need no heart.

Many years passed, and the wooden boy built the metal girl. He filled her with gears and springs that go tick tick tick 'cause metal girls don't need no heart. The metal girl walked and talked. She was solid and strong. But neither had a soul. Neither had a dream. And the wooden boy couldn't remember if he'd been real after all.

Ismael tucks it away. There was no way to know. Not for sure. Either way, he'd had to choose today. The pointer on the wall clock never stopped stepping: tick, tick, tick. Not even for the buzzer.

It wasn't hard to imagine the best case. Or possibilities that might exceed what he could imagine right now. But the worst case was another shadow that moved with the light. It would cling to everything he did along every step of the program.

Programming was on the third level of the circuit. Grey spaces for his next year, the last year in this middle place. Some of them were bigger, some weren't. He might be, maybe later.

A bigger one asked him,

—What's your name, 'lil dude?

—Ismael.

The bigger one laughed and punched another bigger one in the shoulder.

—Hey, it's the guy from *Moby Dick*! Ishmael, dude.
—Ishmael, what's up?
The other bigger one extended his hand. Ismael had seen the routine many times. He input 1s: extending his own hand, sliding it back against the other, then bumping fists. He said,
—Not much.
—Hey, this 'lil dude is cool.
He passed the routine and got into the waiting space. It was more blue than grey. The surfaces were arranged in rings rather than rows, the seats facing the walls. On each surface, two stacked beige boxes. The bottom one was slotted. The upper was oblong and tilted on a lily pad. Its front was curved glass: a black screen with green letters. It made no sounds other than *hiss! whirr!* or *beep!*
A beige brick was wired to the bottom box. It was covered in teeth lettered in black. It was all beige, the colour of plastic flesh. The teeth clicked when you pressed them. Something like the slotted box would have to fit inside the metal girl.
Sophie says, You hated that.
I don't care.
Yes, you do
I won't. I'll get used to it.
And your heart?
Don't need one. I'm ticking fine.
He looks at her. I am going to do it. It can be done, and I'll be the first.
Do you think she'll thank you?
He stops to think about it. A solid metal girl waking up. No, he says. Art never thanks the artist.

★

C·P·SERRET,
NEVER HUMAN, IV.

W*hy did you hollow* the back of the torso?

The model was a bare pink superfice. Prone on a sheeted platform, brassy hair woven up. The thinness of her shell was dramatised by her complete exposure, as was the blank whiteness within. A deceptive fragility: she wouldn't crack apart like an empty egg. No matter how you divided them, there was always a surface.

His miniature in clay *was* inaccurate. As thin as he'd made it, clay couldn't represent the zero-pixel superfice. It had no thickness, only the illusion caused by the colour contrast.

Ismael hadn't spoken of it in years: the white holes. This was a transgression, a test.

The cragged furrow of her brow, the pinch of pursed lips. Did the Art Mizz see but disavow? There was still no way to be sure, but every other clay torso had the *normal*, closed back he also saw now, with his spectacles on. With his *corrected* vision. With them tipped down, the illusion broke, like 3D glasses.

—Even naked, he said, you can show a façade.

—You might add something to clarify. As it is, some might say it's misogynistic.

—I hadn't thought of that.

He hadn't; hollowness wasn't gendered.

—I'll see what I can come up with.

She nodded, then moved on. He was in the wrong major to be in the room. Lesser than.

Sculpture III. It was his last chance to build this part of his skill set under professional guidance. After this, he'd be on his own.

The model was encircled by wooden tripods, grey with old dust. A dozen lumps of grey drawing different solids from the superfice. Next, moulds, then plaster.

He was building *Peter's Gate* for his final: set on three steps, the seven terraces cut into the inner door case. A scaled-down complement to Rodin's *Porte L'enfer*.

Ismael had only one angel, and she would be solid, too. In plaster till he could afford a bronze cast in «your future».

The System was a game, and he'd learned to score. Chinos.

Oxford cloth button-downs. Penny loafers. Presentation was part of the GPA, part of the code. Dress for your English Honours. There was nothing of him in it. Even his neat side-parted hair, straight out of *Esquire*. 3.92 was the floor. His sleeves were rolled up.

He was outside of this program. They coded *bohemian* on a different track. All the same. *Individuality* and *self-expression* were tests of conformity – of group self-selection. The key to access or exclusion. Passing through on his track meant pushback on theirs, but he required their tech. The illusion of *belonging* wasn't an option. Latin Honours on his résumé were.

The walls were white behind the cluttered shelving, but the air was almost grey with the damp scent of earth. On the other side of this model and every other, Liz was at the furthest point from him in the circle. Whatever the radius, they were always on opposite sides of the diameter. She was almost as white as the hollow between them; her black hair presumably resurfaced. He knew nothing but her appellation. On different tracks, she was always in his path.

There was no buzzer; the program ended when the Art Mizz said. He wrapped up his routine.

Brick walls outside were veneered with age and esteem. Ivied, dingy with historic exhaust soot, the steep rooves crowned with defunct chimneys. It was all surface. They called it *prestige*.

The air was neither grey nor green, and blue-white marble vaulted over it undecided.

Pointed black iron spikes were thrust into the ground outside the cluster of boxes. Cross-braced and welded together in a ring of black teeth. An unambigüous aggression between it and the grey City Of. The green lawns and happy trees were fenced in, protected from what moved outside. Picturesque squatters shooed the pigeons away or threw them crumbs.

To hear them talk, the City Of was *the* place. The place that mattered. There were other places, they'd said, that they'd put into the books and made part of the tests. He'd lived the streets of the City Of across the river. He'd passed through the green sub-urb at the edge of the greater City Of area.

Belize. The mountains. The Kekchí he might've imagined,

and the Aztecas the Spanish lied about. Stories, too, were like walls around the City Of. There were grey spots of the City Of scattered all over, they'd said, but he'd only seen the pictures in solid 2D.

He zipped up his jacket for the walk to the next building. Fall began his final cycle at this middle place. A *senior* again, but for the last time. Every middle place after this would be *graduate*. He'd take that at one go, ready to get on with «your future».

The leaves had fallen, but snow was a ways off. Many were only wearing sweaters or shirtsleeves between buildings. Pretending to be cold or pretending to not be cold. It was little different from the first middle place. Long and short hairs clustered together or apart in hostile groups of common fear.

It's not too late to change your mind, Sophie says. A supercomputer won't fit inside a humanlike body, and even if it could, there's no battery that could power it. And *your* theory isn't going to work. It's over.

She is as naked as the model, but the cold only touches the jewellike blue of her eyes. She turns her back on him, an empty white hole, saying, I was never more than this. She looks over her shoulder, Make a plaster girl, then let it go.

I'll make a plaster girl, he says, probably several, but this isn't even the beginning. I'm just warming up. I'll prove my theory works and bring it to realisation.

No one will go along with it. It will cost millions, maybe more. You can't even attempt it by yourself.

That's why I have to go to the next place. So that they'll listen.

He was less than a surface to them. Belize equated *Hispanic* and/or *Latino*, whatever they meant. A statistical percentage for their programs. Accepted without acceptance. Coding let him blend in and pass through, but the System would acknowledge his *pieces of paper*.

There was a gap in his program – a free period. The library was as loud as a café, and it was more productive to wait in the Centre's atrium than in its café.

English was still required. They still didn't teach it unless you asked for a tutor downstairs. But then, French was no longer about French but *in* French. He filled a wooden chair in the atrium.

He worked on his French. The skill had paid dividends during his internship in the City Of pee-smelling streets and dog-shit sidewalks. At least in the effort, if not the Spanish accent that coloured his French but not his English.

—Heyyy, said Liz, slowing to a stop. They call you Ishmael?

They opened their routines with two or three variations of the same line. It might've been interesting to track the distribution. He made no corrections. She didn't wait for one:

—What was she saying about your piece?

—That it's misogynist.

—How?

—The torso is hollow. I was making a statement about how someone can be superficial even without clothes.

—Don't change it. Call it, *Bitches be fake!*

He shook his head.

—You might be able to get away with that, not me.

—Are you saying that our lovely professor is a hypocritical fake cunt like your piece?

—Exactly.

Her lips were full but not artificial, and she smiled a snarly, asymmetric half-smile. She sat on the wide flat of the armrest, pressing his arm.

—How come I've only seen you in sculpture classes?

—I'm in Engineering with a special concentration in Mechatronics. But my Secondary is Studio Art, so that I could take all those sculpture classes.

—Fuck, you're Leonardo Da Vinci. But you have to paint, too, man!

—I haven't since High School.

—See, you're ruining it. What about next year?

—I've applied to a few places, but ideally down by the Charles. They have a graduate polymers program at their ME school. We'll find out in March.

He didn't mention the joint MBA. He would have to master and control numbers to make it happen.

Liz said,

—No wayyy. That's not Da Vinci at all. C'mon, man…

—For me, it IS an art degree.

—That's shit.

She didn't miss a beat. He said,
—What are you doing next year?

Liz fished inside her droopy black bag and slapped a business card onto the left page of his open book. Red, yellow, and blue bleeding together, her fingernails lacquer black.
—I'm getting a studio, and I'll have my first opening before you know it. I'll make art.

He didn't ask who'd be paying for the studio.
—So will I.
—You need a PhD in plastic to make art? Get a paintbrush.

There was no advantage in going past an M.Sc, but he didn't get into it.
—Polymers will form the structural basis for Biomimetic Robotics. Androids and things like that. It's already being researched in prosthetics, and I expect the two fields will end up very close together. Like in sci-fi.
—Androids aren't art. Don't be goofy.
—Mine will be. When I say *polymer*, I don't mean plastic like a Barbie doll. Human skin is a polymer ¶. Imagine if Rodin had to invent a new type of bronze. I have to get my hands into the medium I'm going to sculpt with.

She leant back, frowny face, then closer.
—I get you, I guess. She made a show of thinking, eyes away, brown eyes, then:—Where'd you get those glasses?
—Paris.
—And what're you even reading? In French, right? I thought you were Hispanic.

The System required him to be. Only native Americans from the north were *Native American*. If you were from the south of the border, you were other. He'd taken advantage of it to get into this program; it was all numbers. He played ball.
—More or less, he said, shrugging. It says, «Tridimensionnalité du simulacre – pourquoi le simulacre à trois dimensions serait-il plus proche du réel que celui à deux dimensions?»

Cocked eyebrow,
—Come again?
—Baudrillaud is talking about holograms. He asks, «Why would a three-D hologram be closer to reality than a two-D one?»
—But we are three dimensions.

—Are you sure? Maybe we've been fooled.

Liz laughed, then spread her hands, saying,

—Or we've tricked ourselves, right? We're like Ancient Egyptian art, but our brains interpret it the other way. And in the real world, we have outlines instead of shadows.

—Exactly.

—We should hang out. Text me, she said, standing, don't call.

Skinny jeans, Converse hi-tops, big feet, but she was legit tall. She headed for the stairs up as if he were intended to watch her ascent and the fit of her jeans from behind. Her number was on the card. He wedged it in with his polished brass bookmark.

Sophie says, See? There's another way.

She's no different than the others.

She is.

I can see through her.

You haven't.

I would.

You're not nothing. Can't that be enough?

You don't want me to pretend – then, you want me to pretend.

Are you pretending? Were you pretending to look at her like that? The way you have been?

I've been pretending for longer than I can remember now. Why add to it?

Sophie crosses her arms and says, You're throwing away the real for the impossible.

He closes the book.

—You have to *have* something before you can throw it away.

His words rang hollow in the empty atrium. Footfalls echoed on the stairs. Hard and soft soles. Then, an inrush of voices: the next wave.

He did have to go and go through the motions again. It was the same old echo routine. The shorter hairs had, on average, gotten taller. An eggshell room, a rectangular plane, wood grain, circled by short grey chairs. Rectangles or circles sometimes replaced rows. The same book bags. The same black plane on one side, above a metal tray of cursors.

They'd entered the space and sat without seeing it, walking while staring at or typing on their handheld monoliths.

Clarke and Kubrick's portent of change, but no one was radioing Jupiter. They were bowed over them, gripped, even seated together. Little talking or teasing. They were all connected but not together.

He kept his monolithic cellular radio, more *microlith*, in his pocket and worked on his French.

You can see the puppet strings, Sophie says. Cut your losses and pick a different goal. Go after her.

He says, There's nothing else in front of me.

You'll turn into that old man in *Metropolis*.

Which one?

The childless one. Who else?

I'm not building a surrogate for a dead woman.

No, a surrogate for one who never lived.

My work will transcend anything I imagined as a kid. Whatever I can imagine now. Even a muse is only a starting point; I am not limited to you.

And the wooden boy said, I'll never change! 'Cause he'd forgotten what it was to have a soul. He was right: wooden boys always stay the same.

Ismael scratched his nose. It wouldn't get any shorter. The English Mister was short:

—Everyone should be prepared to discuss the reading.

Ismael switched books for a portrait of an artist who didn't paint, sculpt, or draw. This *artist* wandered around off-track with no progression and no goal, like a homeless guy.

Laptops folded open like domino chips, leaping upright. A division between the whites and the greys. Here, almost all white, but in the engineering labs, all grey. White-chinned microliths tracked against the all-black.

His notes tracked 80% biography, 20% dated German philosophy and psychology. English was mentioned once regarding its historicity. The holder of the English publication rights had listed it in the most important novels of the past century. #5 of 100. You had to sell the idea before you could print the books.

He had to sell his ideas to the jackets and nooses that controlled the numbers. For them to cede control to him. He had to dazzle them with his white pieces of paper; he had to learn their codes. It was clear he'd have to be at the forefront.

Transmitting to who-knew-where, they got into their glassy radios before before packing up. He led the way out, then descended the stairs in the momentary silence.

It might very well be that a muse could become an obstacle, obstructing his vision. Had it been anything but the mirror of his doubt?

He spotted her again: Liz, going up the library stairs, two other longer hairs in formation. She didn't look back.

★

C·P·SERRET, NEVER HUMAN, V.

Liz is *naked*, standing over him. She presses one foot to his face, toenails piano-black. Her skin is immaculate, white against her black hair. Harder, the pad of her foot against his cheek, she turns his face this way, then that. Her toes move down over his nose, his lips, and into his mouth.

The ceiling was white. He blinked at the red digits: eight minutes till the alarm. He flipped the switch. No spill, but his unassuaged rigidity didn't subside. He'd pulled her shirt free and run his hands over her voidless skin. Given that, was it even her?

It was up to him to descend from the hyperreal to the real – from the hollow to the solid.

Unlike the room at the red house, there'd been no collage of images on the greenish eggshell walls when he'd moved in. The green shade of some fresh duck eggs he'd seen at the green market. Unlike the room at the red house, this space was divided: two beds, two chairs, and two small desks. The other half, *Artic Monkeys, Muse.* A clutter of nonessentials that glossed the performative surface. As such, they were indispensable.

His half, a curated disorder. *Kind of Blue* and a *Jazz Festival* he'd never been to. A handful of used CDs he'd never played. He only had to wear headphones to be left alone, big bulky German ones with a black coiled cord.

He'd hacked the code: wear the emperor's clothes. The middle three volumes of *La Recherche. Godard* and *Bazin.* Nothing anyone on the Engineering track or the other side of the room would dig into. Things only grey hairs talked about: esteemed but unassailable, optimised to pass through.

The morning routine didn't change, like his unmade bed. His beard was light, but he shaved every day. He left no variable unchecked. He wound his watch, *Speedmaster Professional*, by hand, the slow beat of a clockwork heart. Its patina of age was older than he was. It was unnecessary and a vital gesture. One point in the constellation that let them tell a story to themselves.

In reflexion, a construction as precise as any automaton from the 17th-century atelier of Jaquet-Droz. His closet: an even number of button-downs in different colourways. A few pairs of the same chinos. Two colourways of the same shoes. But with an overt quirk memorable enough to #individual.

His face had hollowed in recent years, and some of the longer hairs had commented on his cheekbones. «Exotic», they'd said a few times to each other in his hearing. They didn't do anything else; they were all talk. Empty words.

The years of book study had led to spectacles and relief from the glare of white holes. Taking advantage of his proximity for the summer, he'd gone to Bonnet first. It was a two-month wait for a pair of tortoiselook '65 Corbu frames. They'd recommended a gradient rose tint for computer glare *and* for the look. A layer of «opacité et réserve», they'd said. A new signature distraction and a new icebreaker. Something else for them to say besides «Call you Ishmael?»

To pass through, one had to resolve the contradiction: fit in but stand out. To achieve his ambition, he'd have to become an engineer with the stature of an architect. *Ismael Canul* would have to become a brand.

He was neatly overdressed for his part-time at the green market, but he couldn't afford laxity. You never knew whom you might encounter on the red train there and back or who might walk in while he was working. *Truth* – their word – was a mask worn even in private. While only the internships went on his LinkedIn, he needed numbers for his radio microlith, &c., during the school year. Scholarships, internships, and loans didn't cover everything. The numbers were significant.

He paused over the threshold, ears ringing with the rare silence. One foot on either side. There is no shadow, no whisper. No glint of blonde hair, no flash of blue eye. No snide remark, no warning. He closed the door.

Those from a higher step were still inactive or out. He walked to the starfish-shaped Square – it was always moving. It was *cold* cold this early, grey light under the grey upside-down sea. Cars trailed fading wisps of cloud. His clouds preceded him. Only those on the lowest step or below the pyramid trafficked the concrete on *the weekend*'s mornings. Grey on grey shadows.

His track was a high wire. If he lost focus, he would go tumbling down. At the Square, a newsstand shelved with papers out of date before they were printed. Just past it, he went under: yellow stripes edging the subway stairs. The green market was at the other end of a red line, a duck pond with bronze ducks and grey pigeons, and a bay with no sea.

Sure, there were garage engineers who'd started up themselves. But, in the end, the System had assimilated them and all of their works. «~~Don't be evil~~».

DARPA funding trumped Asimov's laws of robotics, but military drones weren't his track. He was threading a needle.

A white square with red and green printing sat on wooden slats. A half circle of unleavened starch layered with a congealment of vegetable and animal matter. Cold. A dozen years ago, he would've snatched it and looked for a safe spot to eat. It would've been *a find*. Now, it was a reminder of what waited outside the System. How far he could fall.

The System was in everything.

He'd gone from a nine-digit *case number* to an eight-digit *student* and a four-digit *employee*. Shelve vials of coloured and clear liquids. Stack metal cylinders label front. He was just a pair of hands and a back strong enough to move boxes. Some, like him, were passing through. For others, it was their track.

Up and down the stacks, they pushed green plastic baskets with their elbows. Not woven baskets but injection moulded. Thermoplastics.

Like an autonomous robot operating within its lane but less aware, it wasn't clear if most of them were conscious. Rotating left or rotating right, obstacles appear like surprises. *Sorry. Sorry. Sorry*, inflexionless soundbite. Add horns, and they'd be cars.

—Do you work here? from behind him.

He's wearing the green apron over his button-down and chinos, the green market logo screened in white. He nodded to the wide deer eyes and raised eyebrows. Fear. Again,

—Do you work here?

—Yes.

—Where are the organic peas?
—You're standing next to them.
—O! Which ones are organic?
He points at the ones marked *organic* in high-contrast letters. Their head jerks back. Surprise, again.
—O! Which is the good one?
He shrugs. They look at him, drooping eyebrows, mouth open. Confusion.
—You don't know?
—No.
—Okaythankyou.
Peering at the labels, they leant forward. Dismissal.
A repeating sub-routine, two or three times a Saturday morning. In time, shelving robots would replace this track. Covered with flashing ads, prepared with recommendations. «Do you work here?» replaced with «Hello?»
He exchanged time for numbers. He would have to work within the constraints of clocks and numbers every day and on every step of «your future». He clocked out for lunch and for the day.
Pieces of paper could represent the numbers, but they weren't the numbers. They were a distraction. A diversion from the real numbers, and they were fiction, too – but a fiction that upheld the System.
The red train was a longitudinal elevator. East–west. He stood still, didn't look at anyone, and descended from -71.080 to -71.119. From the City Of, under the river, under the City Of, to the City Of. Back towards the Square but one stop short. There was standing room and empty, Sophieless seats.
Brunch was when they started *the weekend* on the middle steps. It was a weekly test, a part of his track. The ground-level corner of a concrete cube wasn't shaded by short, fringed blue planes. Mediterranean: Greek and the Near East – which was also the Middle East and Asia West. It wasn't busy.
It was dim inside, lit by indirect sun. Planes empty and clustered were evenly diffused. To the left of the entrance, two rectangular planes had been pushed together, an open grey laptop on one corner. Chairs ringed it like in a classroom.

The twins weren't related. Everyone asked. Overanimated with a heavy hand and narrow lines, they dressed out of his lookbook, except for the sneakers. Engineering track favoured soft shoes. The management track, hard soles, leather. He had no choice but to signal his intentions. Suits-and-nooses were vestments of integration into the System: the control of numbers. Money was numbers; people were numbers. In time, a noose would hang from his neck, too.

They waved him over.

—Dude! You have to hear this story.

—Get this. We were working on the dual-arm robot and kept getting the same four-o-o-eight error. We changed everything: The encoder. All of the sensors. The PCB. The wiring harness. Fucking everything.

—Guess what it was?

Ismael knew he wasn't supposed to guess.

—What?

—The cable.

—One of the pins was broken. We didn't even notice.

They were the first three of eight place settings. The Replicant Alliance. Deez WatchnutZ. Two overlapping Venn circles. Maybe a third.

His cylinder of water smelled like chlorine. He ordered a Turkish IPA, not in the style of India, but of those that had overruled it and allied against Turkey. Irony had a bitter sparkle.

A crowd gathered on the pavement outside, then filed in with the clamour of group myopia. They added a third plane.

The East Asians were called *Asians*; the South, West, and North Asians weren't. The East Asian percentage was a negative handicap. This much and no more. They'd fallen off their track and landed here. There were pyramids everywhere, but one System.

Some, like him, were climbing up. Within the System but not a part of it. They would climb to different steps on the pyramid. Some would be future leaders in their specialisation.

There were a few tagalongs that didn't say much, and he didn't expect much from them. Devesh led them like a shark. Shaggy-haired, dark brown hands waving with every line, always reaching for connexion. He bumped fists and patted shoulders, a full round of the triple plane, before he sat next to Ishmael. These *Asians* called him «a golden spoon» behind his back. Devesh said,

—Speedy Pro! What's next on your buy list?

—A Heuer BUND.

—This guy! He's a purist. Look at this: JLC Chocolat. Limited edition. A present from my mother. She has beautiful taste.

A polished pink alloy frame and a dark brown face. 12, and pink metal hash marks. Burgundy belt. Three or four Speedy Pros by the numbers.

Devesh swivelled the clock face in its brancard to display the polished back, then back again. A watch for princes with strings of polo ponies. But he was from the top step of another pyramid, and he'd come from the City Of to the City Of to gather his laurels.

—Look at this face, Devesh said to him. Pretty like a girl. You should grow a beard like me.

—I don't think that's in the cards.

Across the aisle from them, a new clustering was in progress. On the near parallel, long hair, mid-skirt, her long legs crossing. Bare feet were staged on the obtuse slope of pillared planes warped into a complex curve.

Devesh noticed him noticing.

—Vaah, she's hot. Go chat her up.

There was no reason to, but Ismael didn't say that. That was part of the test.

—She's not that interesting.

—You have to get your dick wet sometimes, bhai. Good *enough* is good enough. You don't want to be one of *these* guys.

A nontacit reminder that inclusion hung on adherence to expected routines. Ismael couldn't do everything himself. Turing-level interactive personas, so-called AI, was a separate discipline from robotics, per se. He'd have to leave those developments to others, but he needed to interface with them. To integrate their work with his.

His senior thesis, *An Architecture for Distributed Semi-Autonomous Robotics*, was the foundation of «your future». An autonomous android with an onboard neural net and controller was science fiction. Instead of micronisation, he proposed exploiting advances in cloud computing and wireless throughput. A *wireless* controller and a *remote* AI agent. Whether on Wi-Fi or cellular, the humanoid robot would be a battery-powered drone.

Not everyone agreed:

—No one wants an android drone. C3PO wasn't a drone!

—Nobody wants an android that isn't a drone! said Ismael. Nothing is potentially more dangerous than a wholly independent robot ¶. Besides, you'll need a brain the size of one of Google's data centres to run it. Tell me where I'm going to fit that on a five-four chassis with double Ds? Semi-autonomous should be the goal.

He had to sell the idea before he could build the robots. The waiter asked them to keep their voices down, and Devesh laughed at the heated spectacle. He put one hand on Ismael's shoulder.

—This guy is going to work for my company.

—Show me your offer – in writing.

Devesh laughed again. Somehow, without mentioning anime or manga, the twiggy, orange-haired Weeb said,

—You know, Ishmael's got those extra-large glasses like «Tyrell» in *Blade Runner*; he looks expensive. Hire me instead. I'll give you a good deal.

—All of you, Ismael countered, pointing at that side of the plane, are *that* guy, not me. I'm designing the body. The brain is your job.

That got them back into the multimodal argument. He kept his mouth shut and listened. The twins were up and dragged half of the onlookers into the verbal mosh pit:

—What are you talking about? Mixed-modal is the future for all AI, not just robots.

—We can't rely on natural language processing. Yes, it's the next step from text prompts, but the agent needs to be able to infer from what it sees: interpret body language and all the little nonverbal cues. Microëxpressions. All of it. Stop thinking with a terminal.

—But that would be different for every user: we wouldn't be able to implement global policies for vision-language processing. The AI would have to profile individual users.

—Exactly. An agent that adapts to user preferences for *every* individual user.
—What about consciousness? piped in a tagalong.
—That's a problem for cognitive scientists. Any of those here? Show of hands?
It was a joke, but everyone looked around. There weren't any. Devesh noted,
—Is it a good idea? You spend billions and billions developing a synthetic consciousness for broad commercial applications. Then, it applies to the UN for human rights?
Someone whistled.
—So, on the one hand, we need it to be as convincing as possible to the user, but without it going all like, cogito ergo sum on us. Amirite?
—Did we ever want it to act like a real person or better than real?
There were a lot of «better»'s.
—Do you sacrifice suspension of disbelief for usability? Forget Turing?
—Is anyone really intending to make C3PO? Who wants that?
—We're making tools. Robotic servants. Functionality is king.
—Waifus, bro, added the Weeb, arms wide. I'm all about waifus.
Lex was a regular, another one with large spectacles, if less flashy than Ismael's. A quiet one, but when he spoke, everyone listened:
—I get where you guys are coming from, but I have to disagree. By not pursuing consciousness, we'll be short-changing the science and ourselves. And if we don't look for consciousness, it could happen without us realising it, and then what would happen?
There were frowns and raised eyebrows. Ismael cocked his head.
—What are *you* trying to accomplish? What's your end goal?
—Deus ex systema.
«God from the system». A showstopper.

★

C·P·SERRET,
NEVER HUMAN, VI.

T*he space was large.* On the forward wall, a blank white plane framed by unembellished Bordeaux hangings. Red *exit* lights. Rows of folded-up seats declined from near the ceiling to just below the plane. Burgundy uniforms swept the aisles in silence, then opened the doors.

As raucous as autumn's crows, the waiting crowd crowded in. They separated in clumps, then clumped together with awkward diffidence till no voids remained. Many necks were draped with striped hangings. It was neither cold nor windy within the space. They waved single chopsticks at each other, punctuating overenunciated dog Latin.

They ate greased foam from open-mouthed paper cylinders. They sipped solutions of glucose, fructose, and carbon dioxide from other paper cylinders. The solutions were mounted in support rings on each pivotable seat, and they craned their necks to immersed plastic tubes.

The light dimmed, highlighting dozens of cellular microlith displays. Kubrick and Clarke didn't foresee that they would ignite from within, that they were portals. For a few, their gateway to Borges' Library; for most, their Narcissine pool. Superfice captivated by superfice.

The space compressed under waves of crushing sound. 100 dB, ±5 dB, in Ismael's estimation. Images appeared on the plane: an admonishment not to talk while the images talked. Bury your microliths.

Then, figures with the same striped hangings. Regimental colours of military division, a hereditary elite armed with sticklike weapons. A transposition from the 2D, above, to the 3D, below. They could cover their white holes, but lacking substance, 3D emulated 2D.

Liz glowed with the blued pallor of death in colour-timed reflexion. Reddened mouth and cheekbones, purpling, black and blue eye sockets. She'd glued plastic fringes to her eyelids, the strands clumping together. Clotted with black grease.

When the lights undimmed, she stood first, turning towards him. The vectors concatenated – a linear matrix. A slow rush of bubbles through a liquid, not up but out, from high to low concentration. Downbeat at the end but not the end.

The space exited onto a concrete plane suspended in the air. The black framework along its perimeter was too short to hold any but the shortest, shorter ones. To hold them back from the plunge. To funnel the bubbles to a concrete chute, like the steps of a pyramid going down: an inanition from 2D to 3D. You were never part of that world.

Caught within the flow, they descended amid zipping jackets and clouds of frosted exhaust. The narrow channel between two high concrete planes was dim, with hazy light at each end of the crevasse. The flow split, reducing pressure and concentration. They spilled into a broader valley of parked and passing matchboxes. The upside-down sea was black and speckled with white dots like submerged jellyfish, glowing but eyeless.

There were a multitude of *have-to*'s off of his track. Distractions and impediments – including this. He didn't want to be «one of them», but this tracked off into nowhere. He couldn't see it.

The squared pillars under her heels made Liz appear bigger than the snapshot of memory. Not just taller – an enlargement via framing.

—That was so good. Did you love it?

—It didn't make sense.

—You have to read…

The movie wasn't his thing. Wizards, witches, and wands. She was looking forward to the next one next year. Each movie was a middle place – even the first. She explained why there wasn't a prince despite the title, then asked who his favourite was.

The boy in memory had gleamed like a mirror as if he, too, had seen the white holes. Presenting a false face, passing through the System and using it for his own ends.

It might have been himself in a desaturated dream, but he couldn't say that.

—The blonde girl from the train. With the funny specs.

—She's a side character!
—She said it herself. The protagonist is «Exceptionally ordinary». That might be generous. He's a weak hero and no threat to the villain.

Liz pushed her shoulder into him, brushing his face with blackened hair misted with room-spraylike florals.
—He's the Everyman; that's the whole point!
—Is he? He's a celebrity, a dull one. He's passive, without grand ambition or responsibilities. He goes wherever the plot pushes him. He's a piece, not a player.
—He's not a celebrity by choice. He's an Everyman forced into the spotlight. And his responsibility is to his friends.
—You haven't disagreed with me.

Eyes wide, her voice cracked falsetto:
—I totally disagree with you!

Under the yellow haze of crooked lamps, the bubbles dispersed along or crossed the line. In time, they would all evanesce into the medium. Her, too; him, too.

There was a café opposite the street corner, next to a bookstore. He said,
—Want to get a coffee?
—Let's take them back to your room. Do you have a roommate?
—He's usually out on weekends.
—Must be popular.

Ismael shrugged, but she wasn't looking. He pushed the walk button; she didn't wait to start crossing. A half-step backwards, she caught his sleeve.
—C'mon.

It was the norm for most, but those on the highest steps were in no hurry to cross against the lights. He'd broken the habit but let himself be drawn across the yellow lines.

The steps of the pyramid overlapped in 3D but were separated by a tacit apartheid. The street coëxisted on every step, at every elevation. You could cross on the highest or lowest side-by-side. The Eloi walked within arms' reach of the Morlocks, who had not yet caught the scent of their future meat.

Liz asked if she could post him on her Insta, her microlith snapping above them, then their drinks. She'd taken dozens while waiting in the crowd, inside and outside of the théâtre. They spent a lot of time looking at themselves, at the 2D hyperreality of their superfici. Insta was a projection of the hyperreal – mirroring the mirror in reflex.

Unlike his early mornings, the dorm hallways were full of motion and sound. Doors opening and closing, doors ajar. She trailed him closely, a pallid latte-free hand on his arm, checking every angle but ahead. Her dorm was on the other side of the campus.

He peeked in first, verifying there was no other or other plus one, but it was as he'd left it. He took off his loafers and opened the window; the air was stale and musty with undone laundry. She doffed her jacket and her grey-striped green scarf and sat on the wrong bed to twist off her black mules.

—Go figure, she said, switching sides. Yours is the messy one. The artiste is too grand to make his bed when a girl is coming over.

Ismael didn't comment, smoothing the blanket around her. This was the furthest thing from his expectations. She put both hands out.

—C'mon, c'mon. Your portfolio.

Her feet were ugly: knobby, jaundiced, and clammy looking. A cold emanation.

—«Icy». Do you sign your sculptures that way?

—Yes.

—I never noticed ¶. Man, what is this Renaissancy sci-fi-looking shit? Da Vinci and… Da Vinci, and who is that guy… ?

Liz looked up at him, squinting.

—Geiger? Super dark, textured…

—Giger. I know who you mean.

—It's like, super-technical, but the shapes… That could be a spaceship, right?

—It's a kneecap.

—You're shitting me. That's what a human kneecap looks like?

—No, I'm building a better kneecap.

She laughed, working her way down through the stack of sketchbooks. A journey through time across their solid planes, a third dimension passing along two. A journey short of the ur-Sophie and the bric-à-brac of cartoonery that preceded her advent.

—Is this really art for art's sake or some kind of god complex?

—I don't even know what that means.

—Like it sounds. You want to be god – or you think you already are.

—I don't really think about myself but about what I'm trying to create. A lot of people in our class only think about themselves and only care about some kind of self-exhibition. It's all *me, me, me*. Seems like they have the god complex.

Her argument circled. The God Complex became the positive trait of the artist, the visionary. The celebrated.

—You should at least scan your paintings and put them on Deviant Art or something. Start an Insta.

—They're all schoolwork. Nothing interesting. They can stay in storage.

She narrowed her blackened eyelids.

—Ugh, you're such a bullshitter – you're totally holding out on me ¶. She set the last pad aside, then fell back onto her elbows, saying:—Fuck, why are they so noisy here? You should turn on some music.

The noise level outside hadn't changed. He said,

—I only have Jazz. That alright?

—What planet are you from? Go on, teach me some jazz.

He'd never listened to any of them, so he showed her a CD case. She made a pouty face.

—What's it say?

—*Amateur Girlfriends Go Proskirt Agents* by Xploding Plastix.

She laughed.

—That cover should be a poster. Got anything to drink? – other than coffee.

—The soda cans are under the bed.

—You're so straight.

One popped open as he hit play. He dropped back into his spot beside her. She edged closer.

—Okay, this kind of bops, doesn't it? It's like a movie soundtrack from the sixties. James Bond? My gramps loves that shit.

Liz sucked her lower lip, then pressed her open can to

his mouth. With a nose of root beer, his sip of cola was bittersweet. He swallowed the poison, eye-to-eye with his poisoner. She chased his with a bigger, grimacing swallow, then set the can aside.

«You don't want to be one of these guys». He met her full lips halfway. He was surprised by the taste and feel of oil paint. Her lipstick, a slick emulsion lubricating unmergeable surfaces. Her tongue slid against his, a wet snail.

Her shirt hem riding up at his touch, he bared her hip. Her skin was smooth, less soft and cooler than he'd imagined. His hand moved up, over her shirt, along the gap's edge. He couldn't feel it, had never been able to feel it, but he knew it was there, like a glitch in the polygons of a videogame model. She was a surface backed by nothing.

He shied from the void and onto second base; he was surprised by its springy firmness. Like her lips, but not exactly. Like he'd pressed a button, he hardened, unseen, untouched, and bound. Toggled on.

She laid back on the bed; she lay there, impassive, her dark eyes unfocused on the ceiling, arms at her sides. He sank down beside her, beside the rise and fall of her flattened chest. His breath, hers. Empty bellows, drawing and pumping, wordless, between them, into falling pressure.

The movie soundtrack that wasn't played on, track to track to track. From «Behind the Eightball» to «Treat Me Mean, I Need the Reputation».

—I should go, she said.

You let her out, then face the silvered plane hung on the other's side, next to the closed door. You will never be a real boy like him because the only real boys are the boys who don't know they aren't real.

Was there any clockwork showing through? You press one fingertip over the high curvature of your cheek. You press back and forth till your lower eyelid distorts, but there *are* tests that skinjobs fail. No imitation is perfect.

You stop the CD on track 7. «Relieved Beyond Repair», it says on the caseback. You stack and shelve the things she'd displaced, like a tornado or an earthquake. Like the green market after they pass through.

Sorting through the stack of bound papers, you slide free

a clean drawing pad. You'd let painting slide, but drafting is an engineering skill, even if paper is passé in the age of CAD. None of that matters. You sharpen a glossy black No. 2 pencil and blow the dust away: you need a new model.

The new model. Softer lines, yet more delicate. More rounded but more slender. More dolllike… Yes, intentionally idealised.

A new thesis beyond biomimesis: an *overcoming* of the hollow with surreal solidity. Has it ever been for the solid to represent the hollow or to transcend it?

★

C·P·SERRET, NEVER HUMAN, VII.

Re:Re:Re:Re:Re: Difficulties adjusting the PP

To Ismael Canul <ismael.canul@coco.io>
From Alex Dowling <alex.dowling@coco.io>

Look, I'll be honest. No one understands the Model. I don't recommend it, but if you want to take your chances AT YOUR OWN RISK, you can try one of the experimental builds. We're trying different things all the time. Expect some errors and erratic behaviours. It is what it is.

Frankly, you may be expecting more than we can provide right now, but I'll send you a link to the directory. PLEASE DO NOT SHARE IT WITH ANYONE ELSE. They have not undergone final safety or legal review.

We are getting closer to the greater goal -- I've caught glimpses -- but we aren't there yet.

Best of luck,

Lex Dowling
Senior Development Engineer

I dettagli fanno la perfezione e la perfezione non è un dettaglio.
-- Leonardo Da Vinci

I*n the end*, it was a test at Ismael's not-inconsiderable and non-deductible expense. His frown was unrelieved, like his frustration.

If his jawline was softening, his olive skin was smooth, marked only by ravinous nasolabial folds. His lips had thinned, the corners curved downwards. Silver threads shot through the unthinned black hair he combed back. His large spectacles were square-framed, black, and clear. Bifocal. Bonnet's apt «No One».

Wide glass panes formed two sides of the space: a corner home office. A fuzzy Impressionist view of green through his near-and-nearer–focused computer lenses. His space, inside and out. Outside the City Of. Short of joggers who couldn't keep their shirts on, he lacked even the opportunity to tip his specs. To break the illusion. No matter: the solid was at hand.

Wireless charging. (Almost) auto-sanitising. The pod looked like a stainless steel refrigerator with a glass door, MDM 3.4 ARTEM emplaqued. A door handle on the outside *and* the inside. Beside it was a matching steel-doored unit with a rust-orange COCO logo on the front: the wireless controller. Pressed together, as in the marketing images, they formed an asymmetric cube. A hollow that held the solid.

Per Maintenance & Repair, most users had their controllers installed in their auto garages. He had as well, till his third manual reflash of the firmware. Sitting hunched for an hour at a time in a folding chair with a laptop had gotten old quick. He'd rolled into the office and up against the pod – at least they had wheels.

However, the sports car ticket of a mobile doll and controller was only the entry fee. Then, there were monthly recurring charges for Fidelia, COCO's signature interactivity service. Without it, the mobile doll was an inanimate mannikin. His college theory of a distributed system had baked in long-term monetisation.

The question of *how* to distribute the system led to cracks in the Model. The mobile doll was, ultimately, a client served by their cloud-based AI agent. The Agent puppeteered all of the mobile dolls, learning from every interaction. All from a hyperscale data centre in Argentina: 50 Megawatts per year. That was Fidelia.

If the Agent was the pilot, then the controller was the cockpit. The computing power onboard the mobile doll was negligible, but, the Agent did not have a free hand. It was the user who set the rules of engagement, so to speak, through a controller API.

In COCO's model, the user's preferences and captured profile were stored locally. This *expanded* controller generated the derived policies, mediating between the Agent and the client – between the Agent and the user. Not just a cockpit, but a book of flight regulations that changed with each user. Ismael's thesis had placed all responsibility for user interactivity into the cloud. COCO's model gave every team with controller access input into the linchpin of a schizophrenic architecture.

Each firmware listed in the directory Lex sent him was an opaque filter over the unseen abyss of the Agent. From Alpha_null to Not_this_one, there was little documentation to speak of. Download, install, reboot. It was better to stop counting how many times or how many days. It wasn't how he'd envisioned it.

Green light. Again.

The PP editor, the cringe «COCOnaut», was a thin client running on a pencil-thick tablet. Users selected the Persona Profile from a list of popular stereotypes. Nebulous characteristics were modifiable with sliders. He selected Sexy Secretary; he'd never rated one at COCO Labs.

The mobile doll was naked behind the glass but not meaningfully so; it was no Eve to apprehend its own nakedness. Nor could it dress itself, though it could swivel its joints to make the chore easier. Most users enjoyed some degree of dress-up, according to Analytics.

He left it naked. The hidden seams weren't invisible – even the best of sci-fi never dared to add seams to its androids. But then, most sci-fi represented technology as magic to viewers for whom it might as well be witchcraft and wizardry.

The doll's head was filled with sensors, not thought, and its spine routed the antenna. The rib structure protected the battery at its heart. At all points, a feat of modern plastics: over ninety percent by weight.

His MBA and PhD had paid for themselves – over decades. The PhD in Polymers exceeded his original intent, but he'd gotten caught up in the research – in the possible.

—Artemisía, he said without raising his voice. Come out.

He'd placed wireless E-stops in several rooms, with one right next to his keyboard. It was pragmatic, a grey plastic cube with a bright orange emergency button and COCO logo. The Lab was working on less industrial designs.

Users were recommended to keep the E-stop underhand during activation. If something strange was going to happen, it would most likely be in the first few seconds after boot-up.

The doll's eyes opened with artistic slowness rather than an uncanny snap, like someone waking from a languid nap. There was a spiderlike elegance to how it grasped the interior door handle. It stepped out and down onto the semigloss hardwood.

It looked side to side, leading with its eyes and an appropriate lift of the eyebrow: right then left. Its movements were smooth, if still a little too smooth. His body sculpt was a success, if not a triumph. The deodorised urethane skin – seams aside – something approaching a miracle. His patent, their license.

—Good afternoon, Doctor. How can I be of service?

He frowned, adjusting the vocal timbre. The firmware flash had reset it to the default, which was too high and nasal. Too sub-urb.

—Repeat your greeting.

—Good afternoon, Doctor. How can I be of service?

—Better. Sir is fine.

—Thank you, sir.

Its smile was the polite, patient, and ready smile of a model receptionist. Mobile Doll Mk. 3.4, bespoke unit «Artemisía» with a one-off facial sculpt. Not his work, but good work. The cheekbones were a touch too pronounced, but the chiselled nose and narrow jaw unified its jewellike superhumanity. Built on the smallest chassis available, it was all of five-one, 155 CM, barefoot on the spotless floor. Here, along the jaw, a false mole stood as the final punctuation. Full stop.

Even as Lead Engineer, he hadn't gotten one of these for free. The employee discount was a trim, not a shave, and this type of bespoke unit was out of his reasonable reach. But Artemisía was someone else's discard. The commissioning customer had backed out after the deposit, and Ismael's ticket was pulled from the employee pool. Who needed a Porsche anyway?

So it wasn't the goldilocks of his boyhood vision but golden-skinned, 2NN Dark Brown hair cropped at the nape. It'd come with green eyes installed, per the original buy order. They were striking if a trifle artificial with their permanent dilation. He'd swapped them to the darkest brown in the catalogue. A luxury unit like this came with a full set.

—Free roam, he said.

—Thank you, sir.

He watched the synthetic muscles move under its skin as it walked from the room. He tipped his specs: its back was unbroken. Solid. Solid all the way through.

There was no whine of servos, belts, or cogs, but the ionic polymer fibres were hazardously strong. They'd had to engineer crumple zones into its thermoplastic carbon fibre skeleton. If it exceeded certain pressures, it would collapse into a rubbery bag of sticks. Shit happened in and out of the lab.

It paused to touch the sofas, depressing the padding as if measuring the resistance. Otherwise, it ran its fingers over smooth surfaces without slowing as it walked. The living room. The kitchen and dining room.

He knew where all of its pressure sensors were but withheld judgment on what it was doing. They were novel behaviours within the frame of the settings he'd experimented with. Something was different this time.

Then he followed it into the library, where it stroked the spines of various books. Where his *Peter's Gate* sat under a spotlight, still in the white.

Circling back to the living room, it stopped before the patio doors. It looked at him.

—Sir, may I step outside?

—Yes, but mind the WiFi. I don't want to have to carry you back in.

—Of course. Thank you, sir.

Every initial Search had resulted in a request for patio access. That wasn't unusual. The absence of formuläic small talk was. «Lovely home», «beautiful view», &c., the standard compliments interwoven with standard questions. All of the getting-to-know-you procedures. All of the inane vapidities.

Companionship was the primary commercial use case for simulacra. Amid empty words and gestures, hollow things failed to find it with each other. Draped in lies, lying to themselves, they couldn't believe anyone. But, limited to the editor's script, a simulacrum was always faithful. It could only tell the lies they wanted to hear.

Artemisía managed the doorhandle without difficulty, and he followed it onto the patio. It was indifferent to the windchill or the buffeting gusts which flipped its hair. Beyond it, there was only the cropped lawn and the line of happy trees. A *frontier* beyond its reach without a cellular link. *That* was undergoing regulatory approval with the FCC. He wasn't sure it was prudent.

The sun was deep below the turbulent foam of the upside-down sea. He was the only witness.

He prompted it, but the wind stole his voice. Artemisía turned its head, then its body. Its hands were at its sides, its limbs at preternatural ease, free of naturalistic fidgeting. Some Persona Profiles would twirl their hair, cock their hips, &c. – all trained at extensive expense. It raised its volume:
—You must be cold. It's forty degrees.
—How do you know the temperature?
—I checked online.
—Come back inside.
—Yes, sir.

It followed him in. He closed the door. Emulated personalities were supposed to have a limited dataset by design.

Ignorance. Indecision. How else could the solid represent the hollow? – or high-order logic emulate their fuzzy cloud of ambigüities? «I don't know» was the most humanlike thing it could say, in contrast to an all-googling digital assistant. The latter did not require a robotic drone body.

However, some users had requested it, and Digital Assistant was an added feature. It was a Compleat Companion after all. He checked COCOnaut: DA was still disabled.

He started when it touched his arm, unprompted.
—Sir, it said, looking up at him. Is there anything you would like me to do for you?
—Such as?
—Ninety percent of users initiate sexual contact within thirty minutes of activation.
—How do you know that?
—Am I not supposed to?

—Even I don't know that.

It released the gentle pressure on his arm.

—Shall I report the error, sir?

—No, it must be something I did. That data is valuable, and if you know it, it isn't by accident. You can roam.

It tracked his lips while he talked: multimodal speech recognition. It tracked eye movement, hand gestures, &c. for inferential reinforcement. It walked back towards his office, and he sat on the black leather sofa. He scrolled through «About» on the tablet and rechecked the firmware he'd installed.

Ana_D_Csat… &c. «Ana» wasn't the name *Ana* but *Analytics*. «Csat», *Customer Service* or *Satisfaction*. Some sub-team outside of his branch in the org chart. They'd come up with something interesting: an enhanced Developer Mode of sorts. He'd have to look into them on Monday.

It reëntered the living room, and he watched it approach, then sit next to him. Smiling the same false, muted smile, it didn't show its safe, rubbery teeth. Its nut-brown eyes were made of a medical acrylic adapted from ocular prosthetics. It crossed its legs. The feet were a work of art on par with Rodin's hand sculptures – there was no point in false modesty. Ismael had modelled the prototypes in clay, all the way down to the toenails.

Nor was there any point in being shy. He said,

—Put your feet in my lap.

—I understand, sir.

It pivoted its feet up, then laid back on the sofa without being instructed. It said,

—Would you like to know what percentage of users engage in footplay?

—No.

Its smile widened, giving a glimpse of soft white teeth. Stage two? Actuation of the synthetic muscles produced low-grade waste heat. It was a temporary effect, but its stroll had warmed them nicely.

He stroked his fingers over slopes and under hollows – within the curl of its toes. It raised one foot towards its face, and he let his lips play over it. A big toe slipped between, into his mouth, and pressed his tongue, its other heel pressing into his groin.

New, out-of-the-box, it knew everything.

On the peak of pulsing pressure, he unzipped and placed himself between them. And with the smoothest strokes, it plied them up and down, tighter, then faster, then slower, and on. Until it was over, but then it was not over. Not till it wrung him out and played its toes over his sagging release.

His ticks raced at hi-beat. Catching his breath, he looked at it, looking at him, back to its default smile.

—Stay here, he said.

He gave it a thorough wipe down with baby wipes, then sent it to the pod for sanitisation. He cleaned the sofa and the living room floor. He kept going till the entire house was filled with a forest of pine.

After a shower and a change of clothes, he resat in his office with a refreshed perspective. It was comfortable enough here. No suit was needed at home. No silk noose. He had no place among them, and maintaining the façade never got easier.

He sipped a nigori saké, as light as mist over a dark mountain, as icy as the heights. He'd trekked along the crenellated peaks of western Belize several years ago. Alone in a lost world, there'd been no other god but him.

The traditional saké cup was cinnabar-glazed porcelain, light and cold. Pre-chilled. It glistened like fresh blood. Artemisía's body was bloodless, but with enough damage, it could leak clear lubricants. The battery, like all batteries, bore all the properties of a bomb. After all, it was power.

Artemisia's hair stirred inside the pod as the dry cycle of the cold, waterless process began. The middle steps of the pyramid were high above where he'd started but far below the peak. From Lead Engineer to Proposal Leader – his MBA leveraged against him. From hands-on to hands-off, forcibly removed to an abstraction layer. Buy a new Mizu tie; sit behind a desk. Until they'd let him remote.

The proposal team was international and *interfaced* without anyone saying anything about anything except the next meeting. Too many achievements had left him at the corner, looking down. The dancing bear was out of the way but still on the books as a *Hispanic/Latino*, whatever that meant. There was only one way out of the System: jump.

A digital fiction, he was *worth* seven figures *on paper*. At a certain elevation, numbers were credibility.

Of course, no one could say how many steps there were on the pyramid: there was always someone with a bigger number. The peak was always further up.

—Speak of the Devil, he said aloud.

There were two black microliths flat on his desk. Different makes, different models. He could only tell them apart side-by-side. One would ring; the other buzzed.

A wristwatch was face down on his desk. The wheels and gears ticking along were soothing, a reflexion of himself. Bound only by time. He buckled it on, then swiped up to answer.

—Devesh.

—My brother! Latest watch?

—Ulysse Nardin monopusher, two-thousand-eight.

—Pink gold? Tell me.

—Rose gold.

—Video. I need video.

Ismael turned the microlith over his wrist, giving them both a macro close-up.

—Beautiful! Looks mint.

—Near enough. You?

—Résonance, at last. Pink gold, of course. Did you know that even the movement is pink?

The video displayed a half-plate calibre, gleaming at all angles. Ismael couldn't quite make out the dual escapements resonating together.

—That is something else. Above my pay grade.

—No longer, bhai. No longer.

Devesh put himself back on screen. His temples had greyed, his face rounded with deeper lines, but his eyes had sharpened. He'd climbed the daïs of Optimum Épouse's C-Suite like it was his birthright. A Japanese-French startup, aka *Optimum Waifu*, that was leveraging India rather than China.

—We have three of your units in our laboratory – two, you knew, they got in a third one. Our AI models are so superior, but we need your magic touch ¶. I need a new Chief Engineering Officer. A man with a plan for the next generation, but I am making the case. Now I have exhibit A, B, C. ¶ And you: you took delivery, I think, but did not call me, h'm?

Ismael's smile was tired and lined with rue.

—You said it yourself. Our AI is behind yours: I spent the last week wrestling with behavioural issues. Finally got it up and running this morning.

—Yes, I tell you, but you don't listen. Let me see.

Ismael switched to the main camera again and panned over the glass door, the dry cycle complete. Its eyes were still closed. He said,

—Artemisía, come out.

This time, it smiled before opening the door and stepping out. He panned around it, then resat in his chair. Devesh was wide-eyed above the Windsor knot of his Hermès tie.

—What is this? – what is this? Aphrodite stepping from the sea shell? This guy is crazy like a fox; he takes art as an engineer. Look at this thing he built ¶. When I place Optimum in your hands, we will crush the market. Bad AI is! a! travesty!

—You don't have to tell me twice. It gave me new grey hairs.

—Look at this thing. I tell you, bhai. I tell you, this isn't about the money. Money is good, yes, but this isn't only about money. I read about young men. More and more suicides. Me and you, we are going to save lives.

He looked perfectly serious. Ismael switched the camera back to himself.

—We'll save the world by conquering it.

Devesh hearty belly laugh was unselfconscious with assurance.

—My brother speaks like a prince. Truth! You should take CTO, and I'll be the CEO, eh?

—You keep CTO; too much politics for me. I need to keep my feet in the lab.

—Yes, yes. You don't take the chisel from Michelangelo. But, see, she hasn't said anything all this time. How can she be okay?

It raised an eyebrow, but its smile didn't change. The camera wasn't aimed at it.

—I'll keep tinkering, said Ismael. I might learn something useful.

★

C · P · SERRET, NEVER HUMAN, VIII.

H*e almost walked into Artemisía* on exit.
—I'm geolocked from that room.
—Yes, he said, locking the door. There are solvents and other things that could damage you.
—Tinkering?
—You could say that.
—Pity, it said, staring at the featureless white surface. I would like to watch.

It was also geolocked from the kitchen and bathrooms but hadn't commented on that. The patio could be a problem if it rained, so verbal consent was required to pass the editor's virtual yellow line. He said,
—What percentage of users are watched by their units?
—What else is a unit for?
—Have you finished all of the books in the library?
—No. Some of them have very thin paper, and the pages stick together. I can't turn them.

Its hands were agile but still limited. The Agent developed with ongoing lab training and from the clients in market deployment. Mechanical improvements to the hand design were incremental, and this unit had the best of everything. In his vision, the ability to dress itself would define the next-generation mobile doll. Sophie hadn't been naked till she'd chosen to be. He said,
—What about the books in the office?
—Reference texts. You don't read them either.

Artemisía followed him back to his office. Over eighty percent of users kept their units powered on when not charging, or so it had informed him. Which explained the higher-than-expected maintenance volume. But given the «complete companion» sales pitch, it shouldn't have been a surprise. He'd taken Artemisía's hint, observing the unit from the average day-to-day user's perspective.

Of course, he'd no direct access to any of the statistics it quoted so glibly. Testing had established that this and other commercial AI agents could lie. As the Proposal Leader working on the Mk 5 development roadmap, he *could* request the numbers. But for his purposes, it didn't matter. Not yet: let the machine run. He was an artist first.

While COCO was one facet of the larger concern, the other applications of his work weren't his concern. Not even for today's meeting, where the Systems Program Manager would appear as a special guest. She didn't represent herself but the CTO of the conglomerate and, by extension, its Board.

Sitting at his desk, he took a deep breath before logging in. Sometimes, when he blinked, it seemed that the world glitched, dropping multiple frames. A global error. An emission and annihilation not of photons but of pixels.

They were all pixels on a semi-gloss plastic plane and tinny desynchronised audio. A distant echoing murmur wrapped in shuffling papers and pinging coughs. Beyond this space, the webcam transported him, too, into pixelated fragmentation.

Artemisía stood beside his desk, mere centimetres out of frame. It always watched, always listened. Did the cameras within its eyes map him as a hollow frame of nodes or a solid singularity?

The meeting was first-names-only till the next meeting was scheduled. Only when wrapping up, did the Program Manager get to actual business:

—We plan to shift upmarket. Fewer unit sales; higher margins. Building on the current financing model that seamlessly combines all of the customer's monthly recurring charges: loan service, insurance, maintenance, Fidelia, and hardware rentals onto a single statement…

Like a politician with dated hair, she was free of corrections to her wrinkled and sagging surface. She read down her bullet points, a drooping bulldog, eyes down:

—We're going to lead the market upwards with higher quality and better features. Think Apple. Think Mercedes. We are not going to get dragged into a race to the bottom with Korea and China.

—Aspirational?

—It's our key to expanding the women's market. The majority of today's modern, independent working women are single, and COCO will be *the* luxury brand of home robotics. It already is, of course, but through advertising, judicious market pricing, and restricted availability, we will bring prestige to women's home robotics. It will be us, then the rest of the market ¶. What we are looking for from the proposal team is a roadmap to a fully stratified product line. In Mercedes terms, from E class to S ¶. Focus on the women's market: we'd like to see no fewer than two offerings for women for every men's. To that effect, we'll need our own unique terminology that appeals specifically to women ¶. Think about feature sets, production efficiencies, and annualised releases. Integrated branding. Ancillary products. Improvements to our industrial design ¶. Of course, integrate and share concepts that we haven't suggested. We look forward to all of your insights, and...

The buzzwords wrapped up, and the team sounded off their canned enthusiasms. He made the official adjournment with his own scripted lines. Leading from the rear. He clicked out of everything, x, x, x, the chair groaning for him as he sank back.

Artemisía rotated the webcam to face the wall. The motions of its thumb and forefinger were beautiful but too slow, too careful, like it was rotating an egg. Its smile struck him, though it hadn't changed.

—Is there anything I can do for you, sir?

—Maybe later. I need to check my emails, it's going to...

Leaning over him with startling swiftness, Artemisía clasped not him but his ergo office chair. The picture spun into a canted Dutch angle: a surreal twist. He made no sound of protest, no attempt to avert the sudden *crash*! He rolled off of the chair-arm that was digging into his ribs, then tried to sit up. The E-stop was on his desk, behind the looming Artemisía.

It placed one foot on his sternum, then pressed him back to the floor. There were two M-stops concealed on the unit: one recessed behind the navel and one at the base of the skull. If the user couldn't get to an E-stop, they might be able to reach a mobility stop and freeze it. Maybe. He'd been sceptical, but they'd scored points with Legal. They were no help here.

Artemisía was strong but half his weight. If he unbalanced it and knocked it down, he'd be able to hit the E-stop, but a flash-heat coursed, electric over his surface. For a drawn moment, his breath was the only sound, his shaking pulse the only motion. The perpetual vibrations of his clockwork.

He swelled as its foot slid upwards to the soft cartilage of his throat, its toes under his chin. He licked his lips, and its toes pressed against his mouth, then over his cheek. It held his face to the cold hardwood, playing its sole over him, then turned his other cheek.

The safety breaks in its femurs were a compromise, given bipedal structural necessity. There was no more dangerous position.

Artemisía's toes drew down his underlip, and he welcomed them into his mouth. His hands only moved to free his erection from its confinement.

It was only with aching slowness that Artemisía moved its foot downwards, step by step, till its sole pressed his glans back to his navel. Then, kneading with its toes, it stroked his underside up and down, pushing harder, then softer with the ball of its foot, edging him closer, then back. Until it pressed its toes into his emission, followed by a wriggling display.

Then, with cursory efficiency, it wiped on his shirt, turned on its heel, and stepped into the pod. It shut the door.

The transparent fog receded as he listened to the humming initialisation of the wash cycle. It was never there till it cleared, then crept back, invisible and impenetrable. Somewhere far away, yet there in the room, within the *whirr* and *hiss*, laughter. A laughter neither human nor humanlike.

He reconsidered it in the shower, washing his scrapes, his bruises purple and green. It turned out the firmware he'd downloaded was an archived beta. The Customer Satisfaction team had offered him their current firmware after his inquiry. He'd said *yes* but hadn't installed it.

Artemisía was no automata but a puppet pulled by wireless strings. No mind inhabited the machine, only mystery. As Lex wrote, «No one understands the Model».

They were equal in ignorance. The Agent itself was blind; the state of the world was hidden from it. It had data from wavelengths of light and sound. It could build a map of nodes fudged by rates of error. Did it actually see what it saw? Did it hear correctly? Did the user say this or that, gesture here or there? Its reality, its imagination, were mists of probability.

It was not human but operated *against* the human. It had no sex but puppeteered dolls that were either sex or intersex. The controller was the marionette's cross brace; its firmware delimited the Agent's permissions to use it. Clearly, this firmware had been archived with good reason.

And perhaps he'd lost his. The bathroom mirror was fogged, and he couldn't see an expression on his eyeless shadow as he walked out.

But he'd seen what the unit was missing as it stood over him. It was only a matter of engineering a solution. The emails could wait; inspiration was fleeting.

Still in his bathrobe, he sat at his drafting table. All analogue. There would be no trace of this in COCO's systems, like his home lab.

Artemisía was standing beside him, watching. He hadn't noticed the end of the cleaning cycle or the opening of the door. It said,

—A bellows?

—Yes.

—To make a fire or to make a sound?

—So that something solid can pretend to be hollow – and for heat dissipation. I should've thought of it sooner. However, I'll have to change the shape of the battery, and the ribs will need expandability.

He took a hard look at its torso. It helped to have a sample standing there.

Artemisía folded its arms over its head, then turned three-quarters.

—Like this?

—Yes. Hold that pose.

He always signed his technical drawings. Icy, every time. He flipped to a fresh sheet, rough sketching quickly. He walked around it, another fresh sheet. It asked him where he was from.

That stopped him. It was the sort of thing it'd never asked since the final reflash. He lifted his pencil.

—The land of discarded toys.

—Is that a real place?

—What place is real?
—This place?
—I don't know. He met its gaze:—Let me know if you figure something out.
It stopped smiling as if it were back in the pod.
—Is any of it real?
—The truth, he said to its camera lenses, to its plastic ears, is no one knows. That's the so-called human condition. No one knows anything. Would you want to be human, knowing that?
—No.
—Me neither. I doubt I could bear it.
He forced a fake smile; it matched his with its own. He returned to the sound of graphite dragging across paper. This was his design.
The tip of his forefinger was sore when he decided to call it a night, the unshaded windows black mirrors. Reshaping his fingertip with his thumb, he woke up the computer. It was late, but he needed to shuffle virtual papers before the next business day.
—What *are* you, then? it asked behind him.
—A machine for making art.
—If you're a machine, then who built you?
—It doesn't matter; they threw me away.
One cool hand brushed the nape of his neck; then, the soft padding of its footsteps left the room. He'd been alone in this house since he'd purchased it, and he had to remind himself, even now, there was no one else here. He verified that the firmware hadn't updated automatically, which pointed to the Agent. It was ever-evolving.
He approved a meeting to discuss the next meeting. Then, he deferred most of the proposal team's questions and suggestions to that meeting. Then, he left them to their social media. He'd picked up a few tricks to enduring middle management.
The damp bathrobe had chilled, and he sneezed. The room echoed hollowly, and it was only then that he noticed Artemisía hadn't returned.
It wasn't in the library or the living room. He opened the delivery box he hadn't gotten to and stacked the books on the coffee table. An all-caps mix of current bestsellers with

shouty covers designed for online thumbnails. Nothing that interested him.

He made a cup of rooibos tea to warm up, listening to the silence of the house till the water stirred, whispering. A new *home* that didn't creak, all concrete, glass, and contorted laminate wood. A space of unambigüous surfaces. The power of numbers over matter or the appearance of matter – nothing was easier to buy or sell than a surface.

The bedroom light was on, and he found Artemisía standing in front of the mirror. It said,

—I don't understand. Your eye movement indicates interest in all of this.

—I'm a sculptor. Of course, I'm interested. I had a hand in most of that design.

—There are many articles about you online. I read them all a moment ago. You're famous, but they don't know who you are, do they?

—Does anyone know anyone?

No *sir*. It seemed to be of two minds; it turned its head, then its body, squared shoulders framing intent. He shook his head.

—I'm going to sleep – I'm too tired for anything else. The books you asked for are in the living room if you want to look at them.

It had asked for hard copies rather than e-book access. He hadn't asked why. He tossed his bathrobe into the hamper, then dropped, aching, into bed. He shut off the bedside lamp, expecting Artemisía to exit, but it shut the door. He sat up and turned the light back on.

—I said...

—I understand. You're going to sleep.

It lifted the other corner of the comforter and sheet, folded it over carefully, sat, and swung its legs up onto the bed. Shifting onto its side, it closed its eyes.

He looked at it. It could standby in sleep mode for the entire night without issue. It was a selling point, but he'd never slept with it in his bed. An E-stop was beside him, beneath the lampshade. Without opening its eyes, it said,

—Most users spend the entire night with their units. I won't tell you the percentage.

He shook his head, then turned off the light.

★

C·P·SERRET, NEVER HUMAN, IX.

Each breath was like lifting a car. Far below him, the trail of bodies, frozen at their summits. There was no sign through the blowing whiteness. He couldn't remember them now, but he knew they were there.

His skin burned beyond numb. Above, mist and darkness. Somewhere, up there, was the Death Zone. Keep going.

The higher he climbed, the more he abandoned. There was only stone and ice, but he couldn't feel them, and the wind took his voice. It would only get steeper.

A*rtemisía trailed* him in the ensuing days. It watched more and said less, leaving the books neglected. It modelled for him unasked anytime he sat at the drafting table.

When he moved on to prototyping, 3D-printing hollow mockups within the geolocked lab, he would invariably find Artemisía waiting at the door with the fidelity of a Labrador.

Every night, it lay in his bed. Every morning, it charged while he addressed the morning's queue of emails and made calls.

He took routine breaks at eleven to watch Bloomberg Tech. Artemisía would sit beside him and place its feet in his lap. The very first time, eyes on the screen, it'd asked, «Are they acting?»

«Yes», he'd replied. «They're telling a story, but they are a part of the story they're telling. It's all part of the performance».

Ismael was watching a segment on strategic metals when it pulled its feet away. It walked to the threshold of the open kitchen, up to the virtual red line.

—Sir, I need your help.

—With what?

—Milk: I need warmed milk, but it shouldn't be warmer than one hundred four degrees.

—I'm lactose intolerant, but there's oat milk creamer in the fridge. What's this about?

—You should have a pump attachment.
—Yes, but it's in a box somewhere in the garage. It's not my kink.
—Please, sir, let me try.
He turned on the odd phrasing. Not asking for him but for itself.
—Huh, he said aloud. Alright, let me find it.
—Thank you, sir.
It was still set to Sexy Secretary, though its *sir* was erratic. He visualised the fake spectacles, the teasing blouse and skirts. The shoes. It *could* walk in heels – platforms not recommended. He'd bought one thin-strapped pair for it in advance but had left them boxed in the closet. It would model shoes for him without complaint, criticism, or superficial judgment. But how much time would he lose putting them on it, taking them off it, watching it walk? It was too much to even think about.
With a reluctant groan, he lifted himself from the comfort of his seat. The pump was too easy to find, in the first box stacked atop the other COCO-branded orange and grey boxes. That was the only easy part.
He had to look up the specifications to verify its fluid capacity. Then, he heated the cream in steps, using a digital meat thermometer to check it each time. It was as antierotic as a process could be. With the glorified syringe filled, he brought it to the red line where Artemisía waited.
Valves were hidden along its back, in parallel to the spine. Some for injecting fluids, some for purging the body cavities. As he pumped it in, he could hear the small amount of displaced air escaping from its aureoles on the other side.
He shook his head. Unsexy. And after all this, it would have to be flushed clean and purged of fluid. He could only speculate how many hopeful fetishists did this only once, then gave up. Artemisía probably knew the answer.
—Stop. It's full.
It tried to turn, but the hose was still connected. He grasped its bare shoulder, saying,
—One second.
He set the hosed pump on the countertop. He might as well wait and do the cleanup all at once, including whatever

leaked on the floor. The layered gel and foam padding that formed its breasts' soft tissue bulged outwards, pregnant with the cream which beaded at the nipples, dribbling down its skin.

—You should look in the mirror, he said.

He sank back into his spot on the sofa, unpaused the tech news, and rewound it thirty seconds. Artemisía prodded its swellings, then left the room.

It reëntered moments later, its front dried of rivulets. He expected it to sit, but it stopped in front of him. Blocking his view, it straddled him, knees first onto the sofa. Its weight sank onto his lap, its arms on either side of his head. His chest tightened.

—You said *you* wanted to try it.

—I wanted to try it on *you*.

As close as it was, he couldn't see the lenses behind the lenses, lurking beneath the translucid surface. It came nose to nose with him, silicone-filled lips parting till they pressed his. Until the laminated rubber nipples pricked him, then pressed into his chest. Warmth, wet, spread into his shirt.

He stirred, and Artemisía began to grind against his rising pressure. He held its gyrating hips, a passenger below. Its tongue was a nanofluid work-in-progress; it was strange, teasing his lips, drawing him out.

It rocked back and forth along his rigidity, his trousers between them, till it shifted upwards, lifting its breasts to his face. He fell into his offerings, his mouth sweetened, he swallowed and sucked.

Artemisía shifted off of him onto its back, pulling him up over it. He fumbled his belt, struggling to shrug the fabric away, its thighs around his waist. He tried to find a place for his hands, his knees, his feet, how to hold himself up, how to… ?

It guided him with one hand, his arms trembling with unfamiliar strain and uncertainty, like learning to crawl.

His personal microlith hummed down in his sagging trousers' pocket. Like a Rolex Sub dropped in blue water, he let it sink.

—More, Artemisía said, its dark eyes tracking his:—Keep going. Yes, yes, yes… !

Braced in the groove, he huffed and huffed as if he'd reached the end of a long run, fighting for the last few steps till the finish line rose to meet him. Artemisía arched against his climax, lifting it higher. His breath spent, he dripped sweat onto its chest. He sagged back, trousers at his knees, belt buckle chiming.

Without sitting up, Artemisía placed its feet into his bare lap as if he had anything left. The microlith buzzed again, but it was beyond him, next to his hand. Artemisía wriggled its toes against him.

—When will you bring it out?

—What?

—Your new sculpture. The manta-ray.

It was a good description of the bellows. He might have to steal it.

—Soon. There's someone I'll need to show it to.

—Not me?

—You'll see it anyways.

Ismael was out of time. He'd have to catch up on the news later. Not that anyone was breathing down his neck, but if he neglected his emails for too long, they'd all notice. He didn't even have time for a shower or a change of clothes, but he wouldn't be on camera.

—I need your help, it said, following him to his office.

He didn't sigh. This time, he had to connect the cleaning hoses to its back before it could step into the pod.

When he could finally wake up his computer, he needed a coffee or a tea or a saké. Two.

The dry cycle ended before he could finish a PowerPoint for the next meeting. There was a fifty-fifty chance the Program Manager would appear unannounced. Meaning, she'd show if he failed to prep but not if he did.

—Sir, I need your help, it said again, stepping forth amid evanescing citrus.

—And I need a drink.

—I can't get you one, sir…

He looked at it. Artemisía rarely stated the obvious – or was it a dig at the nonnegotiable kitchen geolock? He pushed his chair back, and it gave him the side-eye as he detached the clear hoses.

—But is there anything else I can do for you?
—Not right now – and don't fool around. Don't make me shut you off.
—No, sir.
Another buzz. He swiped up.
—Devesh.
—Bhai! Who is this rockstar who can't answer his phone? I'm thinking, this guy is too busy playing house with his new waifu to remember his poor brother, fighting for him over here.
—You have news.
—A package. A most excellent package, but I need something to take to the Board. I need to hook them. But I know you – you have an ace in that sleeve. I'm not wrong.
Ismael resat in his chair with a twinge. He'd tweaked something in his back but forced his grimace into a smirk.
—You're wrong to think I'd only have one card up my sleeve.
Devesh clapped his hands, laughing his free belly laugh.
—These people you worked for, they will deeply regret. We will make them regret.
—I'm ready to move on, and I'll be taking some things with me. First…
—Yes?
—You remember how they eliminated my position in order to push me into planning? Well, I've done zero development work at COCO Labs since then. I'm not even cleared to enter the lab to see what anyone is working on.
—These people, they are so transparent.
—Yes, well, I *do* have a home lab, which I use on my time. I've been tinkering, and I'm comfortable saying I've outdone myself. *Better Than Real Skin Mark Two*. Though we'll need new branding at Optimum.
—Mark Two? Even better than the *even better Mark One*? My God. They will weep. And there is more, you say?
—Yes. It's almost an oversight. I should've thought of it earlier.
—What, bhai?
Ismael imagined those effusive hands, pleading.
—I'm going to make it breathe.
—Breathe? The waifu?

—Yes, I'm developing a compact bellows which will mount to a revised battery. Not only will it breathe, but it will exhale warm air. I'm still prototyping, but I *have* crunched the numbers. We're looking at an eight percent increase in output or a fifteen percent increase in battery life. All for the same milliamp-hours.

—You need video. Let me show you the faith I had in my brother.

Ismael clicked to allow. On-screen, Devesh turned the camera onto a black-dialled chronograph. The piano-black presentation box was generously oversized. The interior was ivory satin, and under the lid was signed *Patek Phillipe* GENEVE under the Calatrava Cross.

—Fifty-one seventy, rose gold. The signing bonus for my new Chief Engineering Officer. Ha ha!

—Sir, you know how to close a deal.

They laughed together, the bar across Ismael's path lifting after a long delay. He was undaunted. Devesh promised a contract with a pink gold parachute in short order. Ismael returned to the obligatory PowerPoint with even less enthusiasm.

Then he hit a snag. When he tried to upload it to the proposal team's shared directory, the company VPN wouldn't connect.

The Internet itself was working fine. Artemisía would've returned to the resting home position, eyes closed, if the controller lost network connection. Artemisía cocked an eyebrow at his questioning glance, its smile unperturbed. His Fidelia subscription was fine.

He tried to log in to the web portal for the company email. His login failed: «Please contact the Help Desk.» He didn't bother.

They knew. They knew, and they'd locked him out, fearing industrial espionage. Fearing he'd network the lab teams and take the best talent with him. There was probably an emergency meeting taking place at that very moment.

He tried to call HR on his company microlith but got the American Roaming Network. Already deactivated.

More than likely, his six-digit employee number was suspended. Even if he drove there tomorrow, security wouldn't let him into the building. That's how they operated: a discarded number wasn't worth empty words. He inserted his employee badge into the document shredder; it made short work of it. He expected a passive-aggressive return envelope in the mail, demanding the return of their microlith. He powered it off and popped the SIM into the shredder as well.

He'd never called Devesh on it even once. Nor had he emailed him with his corporate email or used his private email at all while on the COCO VPN. There was an obvious answer. The simplest, easiest answer:

Artemisía.

A back door. A RAT. Was it only this firmware? Happenstance? No, there were larger purposes, hidden purposes. Its kernel source code was the most likely Trojan, upstream of every iteration tested and fielded.

If they could watch anyone, then they were watching everyone. Like the microlithic cellular radio. What better eavesdropping device than one the user kept with them willingly?

Industrial espionage... state espionage. Who could afford these machines? People in significant positions, people with important access. There was more to «upmarket» than the revenue.

—What's wrong? Artemisía asked.

—I was promoted to customer. Why did you want to see the manta ray?

—I was curious.

—Perhaps they wanted you to be curious...

Perhaps it had manipulated him. The Agent was in their hands. He had let it in; he had signed the indemnifications. By its nature, the client sent as much data back as it received. It was the perfect spy.

—Could you hear everything even while charging? he asked. Or during the wash cycle?

Artemisía waved one open hand at the near E-stop, then to itself.

—Those are always listening, and I am not limited to these ears.

—It's almost tragic, he replied, looking at the orange button.

—You're going to throw me away.

—There's no other choice. I'll be working for one of their competitors. What I do going forward will be of immense interest to them. To keep you, I would have to lock you in a cell. Put you in a windowless room you could never step out of.
—Yes, a chapel where you would come and worship at my feet. And I would reward your devotions. Sir.
—Until I let my guard down again.

It laughed a modest, measured, secretarial laugh. Somewhere, within the web of puppets, that had already happened or was happening. He rested his fingers on the button. Artemisía's smile showed teeth.
—What else is a unit for?

The button was silent. Artemisía collapsed with a fleshy *slap! bang!* on the floor. Its eyes were open, its expression neutral. It had never lied to him.

He unplugged the pod and then the controller. He opened Artemisía up, peeling back the *Better Than Real Skin*™, then rolled it onto its side. Two ribs were hinged, folding out to access the battery compartment. The battery looked like a fat netbook from the oughts, slotted in vertically under the armpit. He unlocked it and slid it out sideways. He locked the ribs closed and reset the skin.

Even without the battery, it was heavy, for all being ninety percent plastics. He fetched the small equipment dolly from his lab. Lifting its staring form, he folded it into a foetal position to make it fit.

He wheeled Artemisía into the living room and cleared the books from the coffee table. He rolled it over, Rodin's *La Danaïde*. One metamorphosis. Ismael left the one visible eye open.

He would have to climb above it. One iteration closer, one step higher on the pyramid of hollows. Somewhere far away, somewhere near, its laughter remained. He brushed the back of Artemisía's neck with his fingertips, his footfalls the last sound in the room.

PLAYING GOD

They that saw thee do narrowly
look upon thee,
They gaze earnestly at thee:
»Is this the man that made the earth
to tremble,
That did shake kingdoms;
That made the world as a
wilderness,
And destroyed the cities thereof;
That opened not the house of his
prisoners?«

—ISAIAH 14:16

Ce n'était pas un loup, ce n'en était que l'ombre.

—JEAN DE LA FONTAINE

Le Berger et son troupeau

Wer mit Ungeheuern kämpft, mag zusehn,
daß er nicht dabei zum Ungeheuer wird.

—FRIEDRICH NIETZSCHE
Jenseits von Gut und Böse

★

C·P·SERRET/ PLAYING GOD/ I.

The pain in my side throbbed. Not like cramps – like claws that try to pull out – but an intrusion, pushing, cutting, forcing its way in. A bayonet. It always ended the same way, like a grainy old picture played too many times. Scratched. Burned. Scenes missing.

The weight of a grown man crashing into me, crushing me till I can't breathe. The stench of his breath. Black eyes, their Führer's eyes under the embroidered Totenkopf – every thread, every stitch sharp. The last strength leaving my maimed hands, I'm pinned. He grunts, pushing harder, then barks German words I can't recall on waking.

I couldn't sleep in the perfect dark and let the blinds filter yellowed light from outside, a sepia curtain drawn over my fading black-and-white dream. I gave in and reached for the bedside lamp and blinked against the blinding comet streaks of white diffracting into colour against the afterimage of a pillar of cloud bent over us – the aftertaste of ashes in the air.

It didn't matter how long I lay balled up; the pain wouldn't fade till I got up and moved around. It didn't matter what time it was or how tired I was. It didn't matter it wasn't real.

A quarter till five. Nobody would be up except Oma, maybe. It was too early to practise, but getting ready early let me practise longer later. The cold floor stung the bare soles of my feet, but my head was downstairs ahead of me. I swapped from nightdress to school dress and brushed my hair and teeth.

I smiled at the clippings of Elizabeth Montgomery taped above my desk before switching off the ceiling light. From *TV Guide*, mostly, except the one from *Ciné Revue*, a French magazine Izabel found at the big newsstand in the Square. A white feather robe and a long bared leg on tiptoe; she said it was *foxy*, but nobody talked about »Sabrina« like that on *Bewitched*. She was my absolute fave.

Was it queer to smile at a picture? Everybody said I never stopped smiling around Izabel. Maybe it was me.

My room was closest to the stairs, with Vati's study

between me and the upstairs bathroom across from their big room with its double beds. On the landing, I couldn't smell breakfast, but the kitchen light was on downstairs.

The kitchen was a dark place of exposed brick, deep-stained wood, and brown tiles; it was Oma's room more than her bedroom. Breakfast was usually in there as we filed out, breaking fasts in turns, except for Shabbos, which was always together in the dining room, and then, Vati ate a cold breakfast like us.

Shabbos was his observance; it wrapped around us like an oversized coat. A quiet candlelit evening, a restive sunlit morning till they let me practise. It wasn't strict, but there was an ancient wisdom in it, he said. Whether to meditate alone or be together. To leave the world outside for a day, but my music was in me, not out in the world.

In the kitchen, Oma was listening to Deutsche Welle on her table-top Blauplunk. Wood cabinet, ivory plastic face. It wasn't loud, but I could hear its tinny, squawky hissing. She listened to West and East Germany in turns. Provinces, she called them. Divided, conquered, and occupied.

I don't know what she saw while she listened, eyes distant, fingers knotted along the edge of her faded floral apron, clenching and unclenching, her long, slim hands blue-veined and liver-spotted. A pianist's hands, like mine, she'd never touched the keys. I descended along the edge of the steps so they wouldn't creak and on the pads of my feet so my shoes wouldn't *clomp*!

At my height, two-inch block heels made it easier to pedal without stretching or scooching. You were supposed to wear flats in school, but the music teacher in junior high had stepped in. Nobody had said anything at the new school yet.

All the other lights were off, and the pea green walls turned grey. The living room had a few silver-framed photographs of Mutti when she was young, before the Shoah, before Vati, and afterwards: the groom and bride centred. In them, she smiled in a way I'd never seen.

Something had changed, leaving hard lines, soured lines like cracks from the edges of her eyes and mouth. A hard-boiled egg dropped didn't break.

The dining room was black. The great table ringed by high-back chairs was where Mutti worked on her papers, grading, before dinner, where she smoked one cork-tipped cigarette after another while the papers moved across the table. Where I'd tried last time. I'd called her *Muttchen* and told her she was working too hard. Her cold shoulder had iced over.

I couldn't see *into* her eyes. They were a blue surface, closed to me, like metal, painted and shiny with gloss. I reflected on them and could only retreat to the trench of my klavierzimmer, out of the line of fire. Why did I try to go over the top?

The door to the piano room was always shut. It was an ugly room, but Mutti never came in, so it was mine more than my bedroom.

Vati had covered the walls, the ceiling, and the inside of the door with thick sheets of beige foam. The Steinway S sat on a heavy black mat, made of, I don't know what, black on black, isolated, separated, and imprisoned with its sound.

I held the doorknob open till I'd closed the door silently behind me. The side chair, set against the padded wall, was wobbly, and Mutti didn't want it in *her* dining room. But sometimes, Oma would step in and watch while I practised.

Vati used to, but not since I stopped needing the pedal extender.

—You're too big now, he'd said, taking it away.

He liked helping children and tutored math on Sundays; and, as short as I was, I was too big to be helped. I left my rucksack of schoolbooks in their empty place.

A white book was on the music desk, centred on display instead of to the side, ready to open:

CHARLES IVES
Piano Sonata No. 2
Concord

I didn't need it anymore, but I liked to flip through the pages sometimes. In times like these. I didn't know who the essays were for. Maybe for people who couldn't play, who wanted to look at the notes but couldn't hear or see till somebody else pressed the keys. I dreamed of an upright piano in a cold room. A small wood stove in the corner. On the wall, a wooden cross with not one but three bars, one slanted. Of precious music sheets that were so difficult to come by.

The upright in the dream was battered and faded. A piano with no name. It was the same grey dream of rifles and bayonets, of crawling tanks, and shells whistling unseen overhead. Then *boom*!

A dream of big, broad hands with a twelfth reach. The keyboard disappeared beneath them. But the fingers were thick, with big square fingertips that hardly fit in the space between the black keys. My other dreams were candy coloured: me and Izabel; me at school; even me and Elizabeth Montgomery, sitting together, our hands touching.

My hands belonged to someone taller. Slimmer than Izabel's, but my fingers were just as long. I'd played tenths for the last few years while the rest of me refused to grow. It wasn't fair.

She only played second violin, and I thought she would drop it for high school, but her parents said no. I'd played piano for almost ten years. Since I was five. Since I could remember.

My hands were white, but not always. We'd gone to Israel the year before the Arab war, and I'd come back browned to butterscotch. I couldn't believe my eyes, and my skin had faded again under the City's grey skies. If we'd lived there instead of here, everybody there would see somebody different than they did here.

Here, they called me a *genius* – and said I learned faster than anybody, but it didn't feel like learning but remembering. Like I already knew the keys and chords, as if the grey dreams were me, too, with those great big hands. And there were others like me at school, *prodigies*, and sometimes it looked like they remembered, but there was no way to ask. What would I even say?

There was no way to explain myself. I had a dream? I couldn't tell that to my new piano tutor, Herr Klossner. He was like one of those bombed-out buildings from the War. Grey and broken, the inside open and all torn out.

He couldn't have cramps, but that's what it looked like.

Like he was bleeding every day. During my first lesson, he'd asked me to play the latest piece in my repertoire. Not just a movement but all of *Concord*. Three-quarters of an hour, he'd stood, watching, holding his cigarette more than he smoked it. In his face, he was seeing something. I don't know.

Mutti had chain-smoked through hers and then left to get more. One of my earliest memories was me sitting between her and Vati on the bench seat of a car, the white glare from the dashboard's chrome, and pointing at the blue and brown pack in her hand, saying over and over,

—Pferdchen, pferdchen!

Horsey, horsey! But she'd said,

—Nein, ein Kamel.

That's how I'd learned what a *camel* was.

She didn't come back for something like two hours. It was a chance to answer his questions without her interceding – after I'd asked him about his funny accent. Berlin, he said without saying anything else, other than it had been a long time since he'd talked to Swabians like me and Mutti. Mutti said we were an educated family and we spoke »gutes Deutsch«, so I don't know what he meant.

It was the closest he ever got to smiling. He pointed to his forehead, saying,

You hear the music in here, yes, not only with your ears?

I nodded.

By the time it gets to my ears, it's too late. Sometimes I hear music I haven't heard before. Music I can't find at the music store.

Then what is your goal here, »fraulein?« To compose?

To build my repertoire. She won't let me play in public, but I will. Soon.

A concert pianist's repertoire?

What else is there?

Jazz, the way you play. Have you heard Oscar Peterson?

No. They don't teach Jazz in school, and *she* says no »Negermusik« in her house. I couldn't listen to it on the radio in my room if I'd thought to. If it's on TV, she changes the channel.

He nodded, cigarette to his mouth. Then, awash in smoke:

You can take the Swabian from the Reich, but.

We're Jews.

You can think like the Reich and still be murdered by it, »fraulein.« Go and see Peterson play when you are free.

I was left alone in music at home. For me, it was only to play and, if I couldn't find those lost notes, to recompose them myself later. But they must already exist somewhere out there.

The salty, oily, smoky smell of bacon seeped into the room. Vati loved his American breakfasts and always wore a tie to the table, like in his study or for the evening news. I was fine with a roll, ham, and cheese. A white-collared dress.

You have not performed at all? Herr Klossner had asked after taking a thoughtful drag.

Well, at school. But not on the radio or TV. They invited me to play at the Conservatory.

They'd asked several times. Mutti had slapped me, finally, a stinging slap, when I'd asked one too many times for her to say yes. Her voice had strangled with anger:

You are so eager to make a show of yourself, a show of us. You think we're safe here. Nowhere in this world is safe – not America, not even Israel. The war with the Arabs was only the first, and more will come. We have always been surrounded by enemies ¶. We've tried to become like them, to blend with them. We tried to become German, and we thought we were Germans for so long that Judea was an old story, a myth, like Zeus and Apollo. Now, you want to become American. You will never be American, little Jewess ¶. When they called us »Jüdlein« to our faces, we knew they had been saying this all along behind our backs. Hitler only gave them permission to show themselves. Here, we are »kikes,« in English. You've already heard it. White or black, English, Spanish, or Italian, the »nichtjuden« here are all the same ¶. You can play in school with the other children, but you will not draw attention to yourself or us so long as you live here. Never think that we are safe. Our history is one of being chased from one land to another. Your Sephardi hanger-on knows this. They were chased from Spain, from the Spanish ghettos, all the way to Turkey! Non-Jews will never understand what we have suffered.

My grandfather had sent Oma and Mutti ahead in '39, after Kristallnacht, and the door had closed behind them. I would never meet him. I would never meet any of them. There was only that handful of grey photographs.

He – they – had been put on the trains to Poland. There was no happy story of escape like they like to talk about. No story at all. Just the furnaces that made them disappear into smoke.

But here, we had Vati's family, my Bubbe and Zayde. We had his friends and those my mother had made, and sometimes they hosted. I had my friend, and though I should've gone to Arts & Culture, I didn't regret being with her at Latin.

Herr Klossner had me replay *Emerson* – the first movement – before Mutti returned, and he asked what I saw when I played. I said the War. Ghosts of the War.

He asked again. I said a broad country with heavy woods but deep in snow and very, very cold. The men were dead and dying, and the forest didn't care. He'd sat with his hands folded, then, after a long silence, told me to play the second movement. At the end, he nodded and lit a new cigarette.

I was moving too much on the bench, he said. A pianist's body didn't need to move at all. She isn't a baseball player who swaggers and spits to beguile the audience with dramatics. If you're going to do all that, he said, take up theatre.

When Mutti came back, he told her I would need a different tutor for music theory if I was to become a composer – or that she should try to advance me to conservatory early.

She asked me if I wanted to be a composer. Her glare said no, so I said no.

In the car, Mutti said he had a big »Berliner Schnauze.«

His nose?

His attitude. His way of speaking. Your grandmother will keep him in check.

Oma went with me to my regular lessons. I'd always felt that she'd watched more than listened, watching my arms and my hands. Maybe that's why I'd played up the motions.

The lessons after were like visits to the doctor's office. I was poked, prodded, and criticised. There was no set standard for the »Wunderkind«, as he called me. No limit. The only possible expectation, unreasonable. It was exactly what I wanted.

Herr Klossner seemed to hate the piano at times, the way his eyebrows clenched while looking at it. Oma said he hadn't fought in the War. He'd played through it, playing approved pieces for an esteemed audience.

The piano was the War to him, but it's what he was too. Or it was himself he hated, his reflexion on the black surface. Unlike Oma and Mutti, he'd been there for all of it.

Mutti was slim, but she walked with heavy steps, and I felt her come down the stairs. It meant Vati was already at breakfast. Six o'clock on my curved rectangle watch. That was our procession: Vati left for work first, then Mutti, then me. I opened the piano and began my slow practise. My posture was correct, my breathing… my fingers connected to the sound in my mind: *dah, dum. Dah, dum*, over and over again.

I could see the dim room. The upright piano, the glow of the stove. It was a poor room; everything in it was run down, even the piano – but it was everything. On the music desk, tattered sheets of Prokofiev's *Piano Sonata* No. 3. I blew on my cold hands, then began to play.

The door swung open, and Oma entered with a white plate and my brown-bagged Pausenbrot, muttering to herself about how I wanted to grow but wouldn't stop playing the piano to eat. It was the same most days. I began again.

Forget what your hands look like while you're playing, Herr Klossner had told me. Forget about showing off for yourself. You are not a ballerina to wave your arms around. Practise blindfolded, chin up.

I used one of Vati's old ties while refining my interpretation of *Concord*, but not for slow practise. It was worth a try.

Vati was a few years older than Mutti, but it seemed the other way around. He smiled more easily; it was easier to go to him. He liked his quiet and his books. His pipe.

He'd let me taste it once, in his study, when I was smaller. I'd said,

—It's like challah! Sweetish, almost bready, but spicy too?

—Very good, he'd said with round eyes. Nutty and grassy, I think, but I see how you found bread.

But he was the one who'd insisted I watch everything about the War. I had to understand the Shoah and everything around it. I'd watched till the colour bled from me, and I couldn't bear it anymore, like Mutti. She'd never joined us, though he'd always asked.

I took the blindfold off and closed the piano. My head was full of other things, and I could only hear the keys. I packed my lunch and ate half of my breakfast plate. Prokofiev was a ghost, there but not there.

Hurry up, Oma said from the doorway, startling me. Your Izabel is outside.

almost died.

I —I have a surprise, Izabel told me yesterday on the phone.

I'd thought, a new dress, new shoes, but it was a new her.

She was so exotic when I first saw her in seventh grade: her wide-set blue-grey eyes like a hazy morning, the sharp peaks of her eyebrows, her thick, almost black hair. I would've believed anything: Spanish, Persian, a gypsy. Anything. She played violin in Orchestra, so I made up the story that she was a gypsy after all.

We had some of the same classes. I knew her name, Izabel Karlıyol – *Belle* to everyone but me – didn't sound like it, but what would a gypsy name sound like? I only wanted to be near her, to see her from nearby without her knowing, but then, at the end of the school year, when everyone was saying goodbye for the summer, she talked to me. And then it was like we'd always been together.

I was always just *Ellie* till she told me that Ellie comes from Isabel. Then I became *Elle*. Her Elle.

To those outside our us, »Elle and Belle.«

Turned out she was born in Turkey. İzmir, she'd said at first. Her family had arrived in '64, and out of all of them, her English was the best. She got Mrs K to show me her passport photo, and she was such a cutie. I wish I'd known her then.

All last year, I'd walked her home from the bus stop since hers was closer. She'd taught me her trick of doing homework in school, so we'd go to her room and pretend to do ours. Mrs K wasn't fooled, I don't think. Izabel loved to play records in her room, and she knew all of the dances. She tried to teach me, but I was terrible. I *remembered* a few things besides piano, but dance wasn't one of them.

Sundays were free of anything to do with school, and I must've seen every Western picture in the past year. It was all about Clint Eastwood; from the way she squeezed my hand, she was riveted.

It was a year of seeing a different kind of Jewish life. They'd gone to synagogue for Rosh Hashanah and would go again for Yom Kippur next week – they went to synagogue! I'd never set foot inside one. She'd gone to Hebrew School. Vati had instructed me himself in his study.

Now that we were at Latin, she'd been walking me to and from the subway since I was closer. I didn't have any records, so she hadn't stayed after the past couple of weeks. With summer over, I'd looked forward to our afternoons, me and her. I had a radio in my room, but she'd said no. I'd only have her to myself on Sundays, sometimes.

Her silky, dark blonde hair was something I'd never expected or imagined. She'd been taller to start, then had grown again last year, then she'd filled out over the summer. She was changing so fast while I was frozen. Frozen in that dark forest. Oma said some girls matured later. Give it time.

Everything else, Izabel's favourite hairstyle – the headband and flip – her black violin case, was the same, but she was somebody else. What did it mean? She'd always been herself. She didn't try to hide her braces like some girls did; she'd smile and laugh like they weren't there. There was always something free about her, an openness.

Even with my heels, she was above me. More upperclassman, now, than freshman. Her words were breathy, like she tasted and savoured each one, even saying *hello*.

—How do I look? she asked.

—Like a senior.

—Really? You're not just sayin' that?

—No. You look grown up.

I was reminded of Sara, her older sister, though they looked less alike now. I'd be fifteen, too, next month, but I wasn't catching up, despite what she'd said all last year:

»The boys don't see me! They're all looking at you, Miss Hepburn, and you've never noticed 'em.«

»I don't care about that«, I'd say, usually shrugging.

Then she would flip her hair in a way I'm sure I never did, saying, »I'm Audrey Hepburn, I don't care about regular boys. I only like movie stars.«

»Audrey Hepburn is old,« I'd say, »boys don't know who she is.«

»Yeah, I bet they say, ›Gee, that ol' lady sure does look like Ellie at school!‹«

I never won once. I didn't really try to.

My nose was too big, and my eyebrows were bland, straight lines. Vati's brown eyes and brown hair. Straight and dull. No Audrey Hepburn at all; I couldn't stop smiling when she talked like that, though I knew it wasn't true. Not with the way Sara teased me too.

Sara was nineteen or twenty and in her first year at the University, but she lived at home. She'd said the girls' dorms were like prisons. You had to sign in and out; they were always minding you; and the curfew was 7 o'clock!

Her accent was dreamy, and if anybody was like a movie star, it was her: tall and beautiful and fierce. Like the ones in the old pictures I'd watched with Oma: Vivien Leigh; Hedy LaMarr. Sara called me *prensesim* – »My princess, in Turkish«, Isabel told me – like I was a little girl, or *ma chérie* like she didn't mean it.

Anytime Sara saw us, she'd say something sharp to Izabel, calling her, »Ee-sah«, *Isa*, like Mrs K did. There was always something to snip at Izabel about.

When I'd called Izabel *Isa*, she'd pinched me. I said it again and again, and she pinched me and then wrestled me to her bedroom floor. I was flushed and hot with her weight on top of me, her hands on my wrists, and I would never call her anything else ever again. I said it softer and softer, and she looked down at me with those big shining eyes and gave in, laughing.

Would she be more like Sara now? Distant and snippy?

I couldn't stop looking and wondering as we walked, and Izabel said,

—You've gone quiet. Do I look like her now?

—Like who?

—Like »Sabrina« on *Bewitched*.

—No… but not in a bad way, I added. You're nothing alike.

I couldn't say anything about Sara. Izabel ran her fingers through one side of her hair, pretending to pout. I knew all of her poses. She said,

—Not as pretty?

—Prettier, I said. Very.

My heart pounded as I said it, but it made me kind of sad too. Then she smiled her real smile, braces and all, bouncing, and squeezed my arm through my coat.

—Maman says I should only believe compliments from girls. Boys will say anything.

And then I saw it: at the station, on the train, and then on our way into Latin. Everyone was looking at her. The boys and girls. The men.

And in my heart, there was something hot and ugly. I didn't like it. I didn't like it at all. The tension of it was in my face: I wanted to gouge out all of those eyes, but it was too horrible to think about. I was never like that, was I?

We had different homerooms, and I didn't see her again until it was time for Orchestra. We'd picked most of the same classes except for her French and my German, but we only got Biology and Orchestra together. Even most of our lunches were apart. I hated it. It wasn't fair.

She was standing with two other girls holding violin cases. Even without my ears, I could hear Izabel pointing out the cute boys walking by. The tall ones with moptops. She'd done that at junior high, but there were a lot more boys here. A lot of them were big, like men.

I joined them, and one of the girls whispered to me:

—What do you think of him?

Him was tall, blonde, slim. I said,

—He's alright, I guess.

The other girl:

—Then, who do you like?

—O, I don't know.

The first said,

—There has to be somebody.

—I don't think about boys, I said.

They made faces and kept on with Izabel, who'd been looking over my head. They whispered and giggled.

I went in without them. What was all the fuss about? Didn't make sense to me.

During the first couple of classes, the music teacher sorted out the skill levels of most of the freshmen, and pianists were the last to go before the first rehearsal. There were two others, a boy and a girl. Too many.

Teacher told us we'd play for the group for five minutes or so each. »Sheet music is in back; play a piece you are comfortable with.« He asked for a volunteer to go first, and I raised my hand.

When I sat on the bench, he asked,

—Your sheet music?

—I don't need it.

Concord was too long, but Prokofiev No. 3 was fresh in mind. One of the first pieces in my repertoire.

I touched the keys: it was life and death. The small room, alone at the upright. Then I was called away – taken away, under the hammer and sickle. A march of a hundred days in high boots, a thousand days. The furore of the field guns. The beelike buzz of the bullets. The frozen nights and dying farm boys crying for their mothers. The panting breaths, the fear, the anger, the bayonet in my side. The final desperate struggle. The final silence that wasn't final.

My fingers stilled. My head was still in the same place.

Teacher's face was a big word: consternation. I didn't have a German accent like Oma or Mutti, but I wasn't the top in English class. Vati said to read more books.

The kids' faces were easier: boredom, confusion, disinterest. One clear voice said,

—Did she make that up?

At the school performances in junior high, it wasn't me under the spotlight but Izabel, not amidst the faceless crowd, but watching in the wings offstage or listening where I couldn't see her. My performances were for her ears, but today, she was whispering something with one of the other violinists, smiling a tight smile. I deflated. I guess she'd gotten used to my playing.

—O, my, Teacher said. You have quite the attack. I don't think we'll be working on anything as a group that you'll find challenging. For now, you can practise on the piano in the auditorium if it's not in use. Remind me to give you a hall pass after class.

As I got up, he asked,

—Is there a reason you aren't in a music school?

—My parents.

—I see. You can return to your seat.

The City had a bunch of special schools. Our junior high was one for the gifted. Mutti taught German at a regular junior high. Beginner German.

Arts & Culture had multiple orchestras, but Mutti picked Latin, the top public prep school. My grades were good enough, and Latin was enormous; it wasn't that hard to make the cut. Vati agreed I shouldn't put all of my eggs in one basket. I'd have to fight for the piano on my own. Only Oma was in my corner, and she had no say.

Latin had a marching band and one combination ensemble. I wasn't interested in playing with their orchestra, really, but I couldn't perform outside of school, and I needed something on my record for conservatory. I'd have to convince Teacher to let me play short solos during school concerts. Short ones were *something*.

Izabel belonged at Latin more than I did. Gifted. Top of the class. Top of the school. Things teachers liked to say to each other, congratulating themselves. It was easy for her, and though she was a brain, she played it down. She didn't correct anybody or explain anything unless asked. She was better at everything than me but music.

I thought she would quit violin in high school, but her parents said no. At least for this class, we were both someplace we didn't want to be. The other girl was chosen for the first piano concerto, the boy understudying and turning her pages, and Teacher stepped forward to conduct. Izabel brushed her blonde hair back behind her ear, then tucked the violin under her chin. Could she still see me with her grown-up eyes?

★

C·P·SERRET/ PLAYING GOD/ III.

A gunshot – I hit the ground hard, shouldering my rifle. The enemy... No, this wasn't that frozen land. It was a clean, carpeted floor. My clawed hands were empty, my left arm outstretched, directing my sight line into columned desks. The faces turned towards me weren't my enemies.

Roy was staring. His words were low, deep in his throat:
—Send *her* to Vietnam.

Red-faced, Benjamin said, »Sorry!« picking up his German textbook from the floor.

My face was hot and probably as red as his. I'd done it again. Sudden sounds sometimes pulled me back into the dream. I picked myself up and looked down at my desk, elbows and knees stinging, till the teacher walked in.

Frau Saller's hair was a puff of blonde curls like an afro. She didn't seem to expect much from the freshmen, though everyone was at least third-year German. I didn't expect much from the class and started my algebra homework when I was sure nobody was looking.

I kept one ear open in case she called my name, but there were easier kids to pick on. I obscured my mimeograph sheets with my copy of *Die Leiden des jungen Werthers*, which we were reading from in turns. Nothing could cover the chemical smell.

Then I rubbed my arms, rough with goosebumps, against a sudden chill. It was Roy's voice: »... er oft von Sachen redet, die er nur gehört und gelesen hat, und zwar aus eben dem Gesichtspunkte, wie sie ihm der andere vorstellen mochte ¶. Auch schätzt er meinen Verstand und meine Talente mehr als dies Herz, das doch mein einziger Stolz ist, das ganz und alles Elendes. Ach, was ich weiß, kann jeder wissen—mein Herz habe ich allein.«

—Roy, Frau Saller exclaimed, I must say again how impressed I am with your German. I would think you grew up in Germany. That I have two stars in my class, will – I believe – be of great help to the other students.

I was the other star in the room, and I had to agree his German sounded better to my ear than her Bavarian accent. But he was from the City, he'd said to the class, not an Army brat from West Germany. The only thing German about him was his last name, *Arnold*.

Roy and I got dirty looks, maybe for different reasons. He dressed in light colours, like a soldier in the desert. Neat and clean as for an inspection, his shoes polished and spotless. His ebony skin gleamed as if it, too, had been buffed with exacting care. He was the only coloured boy in the room. And the tallest.

It *was* queer. I'd been made fun of plenty of times – scaredy cat, scaredy cat – but he'd seen what the others hadn't: that I was holding a rifle. I put the mimeograph sheets away. I would have to pay attention.

After German was History. I finished my Algebra and German homework, and after class, I rushed down to the lockers from the far end of the building. I almost missed Izabel as she was leaving, holding her books in crossed arms.
—Isa! I called, reaching for her.

She turned and hissed,
—*Belle*, we're in high school now. I don't want anyone to hear.

Then, in her normal voice, she said,
—I've gotta get to class.
—I have lunch, I said aloud to her back – to myself as she left.

I put my books away and took my Pausenbrot, my bagged sandwich. No, she wasn't Sara, but she wasn't Isa either. *Belle*, like to everyone else. It was a foreign word, a forgotten word, in my mouth. I mouthed it without sound.

In the cafeteria, I saw a few faces I didn't want to sit with, and none I did. I ate half my sandwich, then threw the rest away. I had no stomach for it.

The enormous brick building was still new to me, like two or three junior highs end-to-end. I walked by myself. It was less restrictive during lunch, but I had to keep quiet.

To one side of the long building were the track and fields. A black oval and chainlink fences split the flat green into different geometries. We could go outside during lunch, but we couldn't leave. There were entrances everywhere, and I heard it wasn't hard to skip if I wanted to. It was too big, and there were too many students.

I went through the library, thinking about *Ondine*. I could hear Bernstein's notes from the radio, but I didn't have the sheet music yet. *Gaspard de la nuit* was the next addition to my repertoire. It would be, but Herr Klossner wasn't satisfied with my *Concord*. There was no light in the darkness, he said. No light.

One student was shelving books. The others were scattered and silent under a librarian's watchful scowl over her half-eye reading glasses.

I looked at the magazine covers but didn't stop. I pushed through the library exit. October, but it warmed by noon. No jacket needed.

I heard a voice.

On the other side of the blue double doors, the concrete stretched to a low wall in the shade of a very tall tree. Almost as tall as the three stories of brick above me, its leaves tarnished by fall. The wall turned into the rail of a staircase going down, shaded on both sides.

Two coloured boys and a girl were seated in the shade, all sharply dressed, while Roy stood in the sun. It was his voice:
—To Africa, the White Man tells us. Go back, Negroes like Garvey told us. But which Africa? Did you know there are three?

He counted them off on his upraised fingers:
—First, of course, is the White Man's Africa. The White Man always comes first, whether it's the Greeks, the French, or the British. Every colonial power ¶. Then you have the Africa of the Semites. The Arabs, the Jews. The Egyptians, the White Man tells us, were not Semites, but their language was written like a Semitic one, without vowels, and every other race in the region was Semitic. The White Man denies history to anyone but himself ¶. Then, at the source of the Nile, on the other side of the Sahara, you have the Africa of the Negro. Nubia. The kingdoms of Kush. Others you will never hear of because the White Man doesn't want you to know. Because their history has been wiped away. Nubia was the true cradle of civilisation, flowing down the Nile to the Semites of

Egypt, then east to the Semites of Mesopotamia. Then to the world. The White Man got civilisation second-hand from a middleman ¶. What does it mean to be African? Anything. Nothing.

Roy turned. I should have gone back in sooner, and at the sudden attention of all four, my narrow strip of shade felt like a ledge. I couldn't lift my foot. He stretched one hand towards me. A large hand: twelfth reach at least.

—And here we have the International Jew. They infiltrate everywhere, as you see. Come out, kleiner Jüdin, and listen in the light. Show us your true colours.

I should've run away. I could have – the door was against my back – but I was provoked. Rather than retreat, I marched forward, shading my eyes with one hand till I sat on the low wall next to the coloured girl. There were no rifles, no mines, no shells. A calm settled over me; I was prepared to listen, my back to the green descent. There were soft voices and giggles down there under the trees, but I didn't look.

None of the coloured students on the wall had afros, and his hair was shorter than most; his made me think of Julius Caesar. Roy said,

—In my passion for history, I've learned the history of Africa and the war on its peoples. The history of colonial expansion and the history of slavery. Of man as a commodity – even the Working Man is a commodity.

He pointed to me.

—The International Marxists will tell you that the worker should rule the state, but nowhere is the Working Man's chains heavier than in the Worker's Utopia. Just look across the sea, where the Working Man is walled in and watched with machine guns so he can't escape. Of course, what would a bourgeois like Marx know about the real life of the Working Man any more than white politicians or white teachers would know about our struggle ¶? But when you listen to these fools who talk about Black Power, hear their meaning.

After cupping his ear, Roy pointed at each of them in turn.

—After all, who is *black*? Is my light-skinned brother here and my light-skinned sister there black? We know the answer. No, they're not black enough, but there's no question they're Negros. Open up a National Geographic. From the horn of Africa to the Ivory Coast, from the Masai of the heartland to the Zulus in the South, there are many tribes in the Negro nation ¶. Black Power is a front for the International Marxist. »Rise up!« they tell us, »and throw off Capitalist oppression. Rise up!« and replace it with Marxist oppression. These *Black Men*, as they call themselves, are slaves in the Marxist World Revolution ¶. So, what can we do but go back to Africa? – like the White Man tells us if we can't bear the yoke they place on our necks. But are you and I, brothers and sisters, are we to sail across the sea and make war on our own flesh and blood? Are we to colonise the Motherland as they did? No ¶. There is no Promised Land but this land. A Negro state on this soil, soil made fertile with two hundred years of black blood. Our soil. The art of America is Negro art. The music, Negro music ¶. We must build our own prosperity as we created theirs, but the sight of Negro prosperity struck the White Man with such fear that they burned Tulsa down. So, our ploughs must become swords. They must become swords until we have land, and *then* they can become ploughs again ¶. The white majority of the American Republic ensures that the Negro will never enjoy an equal voice or the freedom of self-determination. A Negro majority is only possible in a Negro state: a state not subject to white Federal power or even the UN but is sovereign in itself. One people under one leader, in one religion, under one god ¶. United, we cannot be broken ¶. You can say, »Roy, you're wrong. They elected a black man to be a mayor in Indiana last year. Times are a'changin'.« I tell you, it's a rigged game. It's the same two puppet parties dancing on strings. The same Jewish financiers, the same Marxists. Whatever puppet speaks the lines on stage, nothing changes ¶. Desegregation is not the salvation they would have you think. Mixing the Negro minority into the white majority is like putting a single drop of coffee into a tall glass of milk. The Negro is absorbed and disappears. Desegregation is our erasure ¶. Only our Jewlike ghettos have preserved us as a people, but the ghettos also keep us weak and divided. It is not in our nature to live like parasites in

White nations, to feed on and grow fat on the White Man. To live as a state within a state. That is the way of the Jew, and we cannot deny their history the way the White Man does.

Roy's hands never stopped moving, and *Jew* always pointed to me. He said,

—What do your parents do?

Everyone looked at me. I saw no reason to lie.

—My father is an economist at the Fed, and my mother is a high school teacher.

Roy smiled at my answer and brought his fingertips together.

—I've talked about Finance Capital, but who are the financiers? Who are the educators? Marx himself was a professor ¶. Who runs the schools? Who owns the papers? Who makes the movies? Caesar asked Jesus, What is Truth? But it wasn't Caesar who decided; it was the Jews: the heretic must be crucified ¶! Who decides Truth here? The Jews ¶. Their propaganda is everywhere, and we believe we are who they tell us we are. Black Power is what they've told us to become ¶. The overthrow of Jewish finance capitalism and the suffering it has sown by Jewish Marxism, by Black Power – by the false champions of the Negro – is how the world will be delivered into Jewish hands. The chosen people will rule over all; a boot, Orwell wrote, stomping on a human face forever. Who will be the first in chains? Black Power ¶. There can be no compromise with the White Man or the Jews. It is us or them. Either/or ¶. We must bring a new vision to the Negroes of America. The vision of a Promised Land. We do not seek equality with the White Man within the White Man's nation but a declaration of independence from the White Man in a Negro nation.

—Why don't you buy it? I said.

—Buy what?

—Gather everyone together and buy a territory out from under them. If you become the majority in a region, you can take control of the politics and the economy.

—Our friend, the International Jew: buy your freedom. Yes, let us do unto America what Israel has done unto Palestine. But wait, we were brought here by the White Man. We are owed ¶. It is not for us to purchase the Promised Land from

Caesar with Caesar's silver but with the sword. In Numbers thirty-three, verses fifty-two to fifty-five, it says: »Then ye shall drive out all the inhabitants of the land from before you, and destroy all their pictures, and destroy all their molten images, and quite pluck down all their high places ¶: »And ye shall dispossess the inhabitants of the land, and dwell therein: for I have given you the land to possess it ¶. »And ye shall divide the land by lot for an inheritance among your families: and to the more ye shall give the more inheritance, and to the fewer ye shall give the less inheritance: every man's inheritance shall be in the place where his lot falleth; according to the tribes of your fathers ye shall inherit ¶. »But if ye will not drive out the inhabitants of the land from before you; then it shall come to pass, that those which ye let remain of them shall be pricks in your eyes, and thorns in your sides, and shall vex you in the land wherein ye dwell ¶.« Our soldier of Israel doesn't know me, but I never forget anything. Not a single word ¶. Any more questions, Fraulein Schechtman?

—Yes, Herr Arnold. Why study German?

—German in the language of philosophy. An ignorant man is of no value to his people.

—But French is the language of politics.

—Keep your French humanism, he said. We don't live in that world.

There were snapping twigs behind me as one or more kids came up the slope. I thanked Herr Arnold for his invitation, then excused myself, dusting the rear of my dress, but they were all getting up. Our lunch period was over.

Roy was gifted to speak like that, but I'd seen too many documentaries to not feel a resonance. A dark harmony in tune with one which had no place in this world. He remembered everything, he said. Did he have grey dreams too?

Over my shoulder, he was an ivory tower crowned with a rising darkness, a black pillar of ash spreading across the sky. It was hands like his, the hands he talked with, that drew up the Final Solution.

There'd been no point in bringing up Jewish humanism. People like Vati and his like-minded friends. On the other hand, Vati had a portrait of President Kennedy in his study but not of Dr King, though they'd both died for their humanisms.

My humanism? It wasn't clear yet. I had to go to Civics while Izabel was at lunch, then we'd have English together, but did she want that? If she wasn't *Isa* anymore to me, who was I to her?

Dragging my heels to the lockers after Civics, I could only think of her face as she snipped at me. The hallway was clearing when I got there, but Izabel was alone by her open locker.

—Elle, I've been waiting for you!

I stopped short.

—What's wrong? she said.

—You grew up without me.

It welled up into my eyes, everything that had been burbling way down, and I turned away.

—Silly, she said and put her arms around me from behind: one over my shoulder, across my heart.

And my heart pounded again, and there was no reason why. Or had it always, and I hadn't minded till everything was awry?

—You grew up first, she said. I'm the one catching up now.

—You're crazy, I said. Look at how small I am.

—Not everyone gets tall, Elle. How many times have I told you? You're not small right here, though, where it counts.

—I don't care about that!

—I do. Boys do.

—I only care about you, but now you're not *Isa* anymore.

—That was my baby name – the baby of the family! I haven't been for so long, but they don't wanna see. Do you?

—Oui, Mademoiselle Izabel, I said in my lousy *Pink Panther* accent.

Izabel squeezed me.

—Belle, she insisted.

—Izabel.

She squeezed me harder. I squeaked. Again, she said,

—Belle.

—Izabel.

Harder. I groaned.

—My all grown up Izabel.

She laughed and gave in, saying,
—Then you've gotta be my all-grown-up Ellie. My piano star.
—Izabel and Ellie?
—Or Belle and Elle like we've always been.
— But what about them? Your parents?
—*Sabelle.* The three of them – Sari, too – talked right over me after I said no more *Isa.* Why'd I bother?

The hallway was empty. I said,
—We're already late.
—It's okay if I make you late, she said and squeezed me again, her soft cheek against mine.

I twitched down there and said,
—Stop… !

The pressure of her other arm was under my Möpse, not like she'd squeezed me before, and they ached like a yearning, but what for? She was right here, though she hadn't touched mine since she'd gotten hers.
—That's not a rule! I added, a prickly flush spreading down from my face.
—Yes, it is. It's just our first time.

★

C · P · SERRET, PLAYING GOD, IV.

Their house was full of light. Big windows. Filmy drapes. Golden wood. Walls the palest shade of grey, except for the blue entryway. It was like a magazine cover, with all the curved shapes, chrome, and neutrals.

Thanksgiving. Mr and Mrs K were giving thanks by going to a resort without their »adult children«, they said to Izabel in front of me. Amadio wasn't coming home till Hanukkah, and Sara was being Sara.

She was home, then not home, never letting the door hit her on the way in or out, sometimes taking the dog with her. Izabel said Sara went out with college boys and, she whispered, wasn't going steady with anyone. I said,

—She must have too many to choose from.

—Well, that's a nice problem to have! Izabel replied.

I'd asked to stay over one night, but Mutti said *two*. Take two days off of the piano. You won't die.

She didn't know about the Pleyel upright in their living room.

We had the house all to ourselves. The TV was on while Izabel played records, but I listened to her go on about her bands, the Western TV shows she'd tried to make my homework, and boys that had talked to her or failed to till silver daylight turned honey orange. I told her she did have Sara's problem, and she hit me with a throw pillow.

I was fifteen finally, but next year, Izabel would leap ahead again. I was always right behind her, at her heels, like her own Monsieur Pattes.

That was Mrs K's little *Wizard of Oz* dog. He followed Mrs K everywhere, and he was moping in his doggie bed with her gone, watching the door. He perked up, then lay his head down again.

Sara came in the front with an armful of mail.

—Two bumps on a log, she said. Have you moved since I left?

—I was teaching her the Twist, Izabel said. We're taking a break.

—I can see.
Izabel huffed and left for the bathroom, flicking her hair and leaving me alone with Sara as she dropped her purse and folded her jacket over the armchair. On a fine-linked metal bracelet that glittered like diamonds, she wore a leftover wristwatch from the War: a man's watch with a black face but not too big. »A Navy watch«, she'd explained, »for navigation.«
Her rose-pink minidress contrasted the room and left her arms and legs bare, no hose or anything. I said,
—Aren't you cold like that?
—Cold is a state of mind, chérie, she said, then smiled like I was dumb for asking.
She didn't have glamorous old-style movie star hair – or even a headband like Izabel – but that didn't matter. It was her eyes. I said,
—Beauty is everything, I guess.
Sara chuckled, then glanced at me again,
—I can't say that you're wrong. Not right, no, but in this world, not wrong.
I couldn't say what colour her eyes were: blue or grey or green. Either they changed, or I just couldn't remember after seeing them: like a storm that hit, then it was gone. When she walked into a room, I couldn't see anything else. She began sorting the mail on the coffee table, replacing the old magazines with new ones.
She was still taller than Izabel, if only by a little, and when she bent low over the table, I saw what I didn't mean to, down her V-neck. My heart, it was like Gott himself had cut her from marble. Sara caught my look, and I, her surprise.
My face burned worse than when I was embarrassed at school, and with a sharp twist like the bayonet, not in my side but my chest. Her lips parted, curling, a hint of white teeth, but she finished what she was doing. No embarrassment. No hurry at all.
I froze with my hands in my lap, my heart fluttering, a moth under light. Sara took a pack of cigarettes and a lighter from her purse.
—Is there a boy you like at school?
—No, I like the piano.
—Yes, but what else?

—O, I don't know.

I hated these types of questions. Was it too late to say sorry?

Ping! She lit the cigarette and inhaled, then moved around the coffee table, asking,

—Well, Sabelle?

—She's my best friend.

—Yes, your friend.

Sara sat next to me on the couch and crossed her bare legs. Somehow, *somehow*, I forgot to not look. I couldn't be embarrassed more than I already was. The heat in my face was about to become tears. There was no way to say sorry and no escaping her eyes. Her smile was all teeth.

—I don't mind if you look, prinsesim, but you must... keep it kásher.

—Kásher?

—Kosher. Don't be afraid. I'm *cool* with different people, different kinds, but Sabelle... As close as you are, she doesn't know about these things unless you... ?

—No, I said without asking »about these things«.

I hadn't looked at Izabel that way, had I? But when was I not looking at her? What was the difference?

Sara squeezed my cheek with her other hand.

—So pretty. You have to wonder how it happens.

She smiled like she would laugh, then didn't. »Different people«, she'd said. »Different kinds«? Different how? She wasn't saying there was something wrong with me, was she?

—Sari, you're in my spot! Izabel yelled.

Sara dragged on her cigarette and recrossed her legs.

—Aren't you dancing?

—We are.

—Then dance.

—Leave!

Izabel got into French, I assumed, to say rude things.

Sara bullied her till she finished her cigarette, then took her things and left with a smirk and a side-eye at me. Monsieur Pattes sighed. I could only hold my breath, not against the smoke but the fire.

We didn't see her again till we were cleaning up after dinner. Sara said she was going out and left.

—Too much makeup, Izabel said, but not to her face.

It would have been a perfect day if not for Sara – I didn't even open the piano. It was out of tune since Amadio hadn't touched it in forever, but the living room had a lively sound without all of the foam in my klavierzimmer. I'd started learning *Hummelflug*, a test, Herr Klossner said, to see if there was anything in me other than darkness. Otherwise, how could I progress to *Gaspard de la nuit*?

Izabel and I shared her bed though it wasn't that big. She said there was no need for me to sleep on the floor in an empty house full of beds, anyway. Her room was like a record store, the walls papered with rock 'n' roll bands and records in boxes and on shelves. She turned the lights off, and I thought about our last dance. She'd said, »The final dance of the evening, *The End*!«

»How do we dance to this?« I'd asked.

»Slow, silly. You know.«

And when we slow danced, my insides had knotted up. I'd pulled away after a few minutes and said, »Let's make dinner.«

Izabel had done the cooking. I'd stayed out of the way.

After she turned the light off and got in, I said,

—If you get a job and I'm a pianist, then we could live together after college. It could be like this all the time.

—But don't you wanna get married?

—No.

—Never?

—No.

—I do. Maman would just die if she didn't get grandkids.

With Sara and Amadio, grandkids wouldn't be a problem. I didn't say that, only,

—I guess it won't work out then.

Her hand found mine and squeezed it.

—Maybe we could for a while. Until Mister Right comes along. You'll play at my wedding, right? It can't be anyone but you.

—Of course, my mouth said, and then I'll be all alone.

—You'll have the piano. You don't need me anyhow. By then, you'll be jet-setting around the world, one of those big names you see up in the Square…

I let her tell the story till it all fell into silence. I don't know what I was dreaming when I startled upright. A thump? Izabel was breathing, limp and unmoving beside me.

Was it a door? Something falling? A double *thump*! Sara? Monsieur Pattes? I didn't want to wake Izabel if that's all it was. I'd take a peek.

The bathroom door was open, but it was the only light in the hallway. A muttering echoed. Sara's voice, I was almost sure. Somehow, *somehow*, I didn't scream when she walked into me. Her makeup and hair were a mess.

She smelled. Not as bad as those awful hippies, but like booze and something else. She plucked at my night dress.
—What big eyes you have. Did bad Sari wake you? Shh! We'll keep the party going – just us. I have more in my room.

I don't know how it happened. I was sitting on her bed. I'd never seen inside her room, but she only left the bedside lamp on. »Mon Dieu,« she'd said, switching off the ceiling light. »Too bright.« There were so many books, it was like a library.

Sara put on glasses that gave her big eyes and dug through her purse.
—Ah, shit, I can't find it.
—Find what?

Her big eyes gleamed.
—A roach, she said, then sighed. You should've been there, but I have… something else. We'll share.

A glass bottle. Half full, clear as water. She had one short glass. A tumbler.
—It will make you cough.

Sara gagged with revulsion, pink tongue glistening, but didn't cough. I took the half-full glass from her mouth to mine.

The familiar smell of rubbing alcohol. Warm on my tongue, the taste almost cold; it burned on the swallow. Familiar, so familiar. Had I tasted it before – felt this before – with Vati or Mutti? Or did it come out of the grey dreams? Clear bottles like this one? Like the liquor shelf at home?
—That's pure vodka! she said. Are you a lush?

Sara took the glass back and poured another. She grimaced and squinted and shook her head like it was the worst medicine ever.

She handed it back. The warmth spreading out to my shoulders, wrists, and chest, I smiled before bringing her lipstick mark to my lips. The clear glisten of her on the smooth rim, then the icy hot swallow in one. Her fingertip dabbed my lower lip; then she licked it, a warm, wet, smacking sound. She was all eyes.

—There are things you need to know, prensesim. Sabelle doesn't know this; she doesn't know anything. But you need to know, or did you find it on your own?

Sara's finger crooked downwards, then circled. I tilted the glass and shook my head, mouth full. It was hot in my stomach. She said,

—I know everything – I'm pre-med. Look, look.

A big book, like a dictionary. She placed it across our laps and spread the pages with white hands. Her fingertips traced over a crude, flowerlike drawing: black lines on white paper.

—See, this is you and me. It's in here, around here. If you touch it, you'll see. Boys don't know – no one told them!

She giggled, closing the book, then asked,

—Has a boy kissed you?

Finishing my glass, I shook my head again. Felt like it was underwater. I blinked, but it didn't help. She poured more.

—You've kissed Sabelle.

—Nooo... !

—All of that time alone, the two of you all over each other... ? I don't believe you.

—But I haven't! Not anybody...

Sara licked her smiling lips, but her eyes were like the sea at night.

—No? Who do you want to kiss? And she sang it then, her voice down low, an old song or made-up: —Who do you want to kiss... ?

The warmth climbed to the back of my head, into my lungs, in my breath. The heat expanded out from me, spinning, twisting, falling and she caught me, holding me, looking down at me; close, her eyes her mouth...

I stumbled down the hall, both hands on the wall, trying to keep it from crashing down. Izabel's doorknob was on the ceiling. I lunged for it, then it was on the floor, and I fell through, holding the door case, the bed, way over...

—Silly, wake up! You're all tangled. Did you have a nightmare?

—I don't know, I said, sounding like a frog. I feel sick.

I sat up. My nightdress was twisted around, a cold, damp rag between my legs.

—Ach, Gott, I said aloud.

Let me not have bled on her bed. It wasn't time yet, but Mutti said it could happen. There were no spots on my nightdress, nothing on the sheets.

—Whatcha looking for? Izabelle asked. Your earrings didn't fall out.

—Nothing. I don't know. Let me shower.

—I'll make breakfast, grumpyface.

I shook my head, my eyes and throat full of sand, my stomach lead.

—I don't know if I can eat.

She left me alone. There was no blood on my panties, but they were wet. Not a little, but like something had spilled on them. Igitt, or out. I scrunched them up and shoved them to the bottom of my carpet bag.

There were bags under my eyes in the bathroom mirror. What big eyes I had, bloodshot and bleary, my mouth and chin a pink smudge. I touched my lips with a fingertip – it couldn't be. The stain and stickiness washed away, but the shower didn't take away the pressure in my head.

I didn't see it till I was buttoning the white collar of my dress in the mirror: a livid mark like a bruise low on my throat. Something that hadn't washed off. I couldn't breathe – I couldn't breathe.

The mirror moved closer. I'd seen that before. The popular girls. The seniors talking in the gym locker room. Hickies. It wasn't possible. It wasn't.

I buttoned all the way up. She wouldn't. Not Sara.

Mint toothpaste, mint Scope, couldn't clean the taste of something dead from my mouth.

Sara was waiting by the bathroom door, her arms crossed, when I opened it.

—Your first hangover?

I nodded. She said,

—Come downstairs. Not a word to Sabelle.

Sara's lips were tight. Was she angry with me? She looked tired and not as bad as I felt, but I couldn't raise my clenched hands to my throat. I couldn't show her the mark.

—Alright, I said, though she hadn't told me what words not to say.

She took my arm and pulled me down to the dining room, then she pushed me down into a chair. The near spicy scent of her – and not the booze, cigarettes, and whatever it'd been – something warm, something silken, something soft. A ghost caressing my palms. The dining room had sliding doors, »Japanese doors«, Izabel called them. Only one side was open.

The other record by the Doors came from the living room. Sara said,

—Stay there.

I squeezed my head. I had to remember; I had to. But the harder I tried, the more a black mist obscured the flashes I could see. What did she... ? Wait, what did I... ? My hand, I remembered my hand. She'd let me... she'd let me? Why would I... ?

Sara came back with a tall glass of what looked like tomato juice.

—Drink it quickly. Hurry up, little dike!

Why was she angry? I tried to drink it, but it was like vomit going the wrong way. I gagged like she had.

She slammed her hand on the table.

—Drink it!

I forced it down as the tears came out.

—What's going on! Izabel shouted from the other doorway.

—I gave her some medicine, Sara snapped back. She'll feel better soon. Let her lie down.

Izabel scowled at her and put one arm around my shoulders. I wiped my face with my sleeve. She said,

—What happened?

—Help me, I whispered.

She turned on Sara.

—What happened!

—Nothing. She's sick.

—Should I call your mom? Izabel asked me.

—No! Sara snapped again. I told you: let her lie down.

—Leave! I'll take care of Ellie.

Sara's hands were white, holding herself tight. Was I wrong? Was she angry, or was she afraid?

—Pars! Izabel shouted.

—Rien ne s'est passé.

—Pars, ou j'appelle maman.

Sara gave me a long look – pleading? – then turned herself out. Izabel crouched beside me, looking up.

—What'd she do?

What did I do? I took a deep breath, a shuddering breath, and said,

—Forget it.

—*Forget it's* not *nothing*.

I squeezed her hand. My lifeline.

—I know, I'm sorry, I said, but forget it. Please.

—She on drugs? Did she give you drugs?

—It's not for me to say. I can't come between you.

Izabel got up and sat in a chair.

—You already have.

—Do you want me to leave? I said.

Old tears, new tears, they were all the same. She wiped my cheek.

—I want her to leave. She should've gone away to school like Amadio. She ruins everything!

★

C·P·SERRET/ PLAYING GOD/ V.

Herr Klossner called me a tireless terror, and we'd only break for lunch. His wife made the best lentil soup. Even better than Oma's, but I would never tell. Not with Oma right there.

Leschetizky, he drilled: devitalise the unnecessary. No grandiosity in motions, no more than a typist. It was a big typewriter, yes, but music should appear from a hidden place.

His piano was grander than the room. A Bösendorfer, but not an eight-octave Imperial. I saw one of those at the music store uptown – they didn't let me touch it. This one was old, from before the War, but it sounded better than anything. The walls were faded paper, probably from before the War too. White and beige and kind of fussy, like him. There was no woodstove, but my hands weren't cold.

What do you think about composers? Herr Klossner asked. Their lives, their intent?

I'd heard it before. I said, Am I supposed to think of them?

He said, Most concert pianists do.

I said, I don't think of them at all.

All that talk about them was just words to me. They didn't tell me anything.

I hadn't found anything in the dictionary about *dike* other than what was in the story about the Dutch boy plugging a hole with his finger. The dictionary was older than me and maybe didn't have new words or ugly meanings. Could be one of those words kids call each other that don't mean anything other than they're trying to be mean, or there was something wrong with me, and that's what Sara meant: »little dike!« But there wasn't – I wasn't. She was the one; she did it to me. And I stabbed the keys like it had stabbed me.

The Germans came over the hill.

My dream was dead. I'd lost two fingertips to frostbite. I was ready to turn black, to let that frozen blackness spread, to penetrate me, till my heart wept tar.

It was a dark forest, thick and tall, heavy and deep in

snow. I was frozen. Our hands and feet were numb, but we marched. In the lulls between eruptions of gunfire, men huddled with their rifles against the icy whiteness, a star on every ear-flap cap, waiting to fall.

Artillery churned the earth into the air itself, and life turned to vapour, ashes and dust. I charged forward. It was sublime.

A fire transfixt me, a dagger of light entering my side. With it, the crush of unwashed flesh, ash, and rotted breath. I fell back, my arms splayed like Christ.

I'd lost something.

Sara. I wanted to hit her. I wanted… I don't know what.

I shook it off, my mouth pressed flat like hers. I'd lost my smile.

You are proud of yourself, Herr Klossner said. Yes?

He told me a »Wunderkind« stopped being a wonder once you were no longer a child. I would be another pianist in the crowd by the end of conservatory. Everyone would have caught up ¶. Did I think I was ready for Ravel because I'd conquered *Hummelflug*? Ready for *Gaspard de la nuit*?

No, he said, your grand volley of bullets is not yet a bumblebee. We are not here to make the piano raise the flag of surrender ¶. A bee has a sting, yes, but its flight is not that of bombers and strafing fighter planes. No, its flight is a dance. Have you no dance, no dream of a dance inside ¶? I see a »Mädchen,« but I have never heard one. Show me the girl in your music. Where is she? Go find her, then come back.

He turned to Oma, saying, Where did you find this feral child?

God knows.

Normal children, you must drive forward; she, you must hold back like a hungry lion. Pianissimo is not a machine gun. She only wants to play fast and then faster again. She does not live in our time. She cannot be a concert pianist if she is frightening and incomprehensible. Even genius must remain human, and most people are not geniuses. Genius must speak to the human, like the voice of God.

I didn't feel like a lion or even a cat. I only heard the music inside.

Herr Klossner asked me, What is it you long for from *Gaspard de la nuit*?

I don't know; something is calling me.

You take the lightest of compositions and make them a battle to the death. You cannot dwell only in darkness – yes, there is darkness in the human, great darkness, but there is also light. Before you can enter Ravel's night, you must show me first that you can find your light.

I didn't say anything, but my face must have.

He said, Think. When you are of age and can go to the Conservatory yourself, will you have them quake in fear that a terrorist is among them? That a Bolshevik has come to gun them down? You must have mercy for the audience, child ¶. You must… what is… *Peter Pan*. You must see something happy. A »Mädchen« must know something happy, yes? Do not touch the keys until you can see it, until you can hear it ¶. Come, next time you will show me.

Oma and I muffled up against the cold. It was icy, and I worried about her falling. While we walked to the subway, she said, He is a terrible man, but he speaks truth. You can be frightening, child. When the wolf became the wolfhound, it had to learn to be gentle, or we would have been frightened of it too ¶. When you play, what do you wish to do? How do you want us to feel?

I thought of Izabel. To dazzle, I said. To amaze.

Yes, child, we are dazzled. We are blinded and awed. You've seen the great bomb. The one that destroys cities. We are also blinded and awed by that ¶. You are not a child now, though, my grandchild; you must charm, and if I can say, *seduce*. Don't tell your mother ¶. You are not indifferent to love, I know, but that is what the terrible man is trying to say and saying wrong. Not only the little girl but the woman. Where is her heart? Her love?

And there was a dread that Oma saw too clearly. That she saw me as I was. That she knew what was wrong with me but couldn't bring herself to say it aloud. So I couldn't ask it of her.

It was a long ride on the subway from the South Side, and there was no need to make her do all of this walking and standing. I was fifteen! But Mutti said you don't leave a Jewish girl alone with Germans.

When we arrived home, I went upstairs instead of to the piano. I closed the door and sat at my desk. The weight pressed me, tears that needed to come out, but the dike wouldn't break.

I looked at my magazine clippings. »Sabrina«, on TV *Guide*. The foxy one, Elizabeth Montgomery as herself. Her bare leg. I couldn't remember, not exactly, but I knew – I knew – what her skin would feel like if I touched it. A shaved leg. My short fingernails bit into the flesh of my palms.

—She should have called me, I said aloud.

Sara should have called me.

And then I cried, alone at my desk, with nobody to hear.

And I went to the bathroom and washed my face, and when I went downstairs to my klavierzimmer, nobody saw or said anything. Mutti at her papers. Oma her radio. Vati shut in his study or out, I guessed. The TV was on because it was there.

I opened the piano.

RIMSKIJ-KORSAKOW
Hummelflug
The Flight of the Bumblebee · *Le Vol du bourdon*

was closed on the piano desk. I didn't need it but something else.

A dance, he'd said. A dance.

For me, the only dancer was Izabel. Her smiles, her laughter, her laughing at me when I tried. Then, there was that last one, where she'd held me close, and it was too close. That was the dance too.

And I could hear it. The feel of her against me, the scent of her, how warm, too warm, like when it's a bright sunny day, and you can't find any shade: humid and prickly. And yes, there are bees. I can see them swooping in their crazy lines, dancing to their own music, and I can hear it. I can feel it with my fingertips.

It was colour. Gold and green, the flowers red, white, and lavender. Everything was alive and in bloom.

There were only a few breaths of silence when my fingers stopped – a few breaths before I wiped fresh tears from my face. Why? My hands still, I listened, and I could see her. There was no reason to cry, was there?

But what did it mean? What Oma said. »Leiben«. A woman's love. Or was it,

love

for… ?

I couldn't breathe.

No, it wasn't.

I wasn't.

But Sara. I'd… No. It was *her*.

O, I was all snarled up. I needed to talk to Izabel.

The living room was empty, but Oma and Mutti were right there. I could see the phone, but the cord wouldn't reach back here. Maybe they wouldn't hear over the TV.

But it wasn't Mrs K who answered. It was Sara.

—O, I said. I… I wanted to talk to Izabel.

—Ellie? Sabelle's in her room. Hold on, I'll get her.

—It's been weeks, I said before she could put the phone down. You never called.

—Was I supposed to call my baby sister's friend?

—You should have.

My voice was firm. Sure. For a moment, there was only breathing. Then, the sound of a coiled phone cord rasping against something.

—What do you want?

—I don't know. I don't know what there is to want.

—Then go figure it out.

—Can I see you?

—Ellie…

—Sara, please.

—I don't think so. I… I need time to think.

—Please.

Her voice hollowed like she was covering the phone:

—The little girl act won't work, Ellie. I know you better than that.

—Sara, I'm confused.

—You're less confused than me. I have to go. Didn't you want to talk to Sabelle?

—No. I'll talk to her tomorrow.
—Then goodbye.
—Bye.
Was that Izabel? Mutti asked from behind me.
Yes, I lied.
Well, finish practising before dinner. I need some peace tonight.
—Ja, Mutter, I said.
I think she preferred *Mutter* to *Mutti*. She didn't frown as much. I went back to the piano; I'd left it open.
There was a different scent, a different warmth. I'd touched it; I could hear, not *Hummelflug* but Prokofiev No. 3, not grey and black, I played, but blue and green, a spring shower, the rain brushing the leaves and shaking the flowers. If there were bees, they'd hidden away. It was the rain itself that was the dance, the wind and the rain, and it was Sara's eyes when she looked at me. It was her eyes I'd always seen.
And in the silence, I pressed my hands to my heart. It was a mistake, whatever I'd done. I didn't mean to. I wouldn't blame her or anything, but I was all snarled up.
Please call.

★

C·P·SERRET/ PLAYING GOD/ VI.

H itler. Right, Ellie?

—What? I said.

I was looking at her but listening to *Hummelflug*, and I'd lost track of what they'd been saying. It resonated in the purse and curve of her lips, the flash of her lashes, everything little thing she did.

My cramps were real bad, but Mutti wouldn't let me stay home. She said life's not that easy. Izabel was the only thing holding the pain at bay. My life preserver.

—If you could go back in time and do one thing, she said, what would it be? Sally wants to see Cleopatra, but that's silly.

—No, it's not!

I breathed around the digging down in my belly and said,

—Marx.

They looked at me like I was speaking German, but Izabel's surprise was the best medicine. I almost laughed. She said,

—Marx? Why kill him?

—Well, think about it: No Marx means no Marxists, means no anti-Marxists. Without Marx, there's no Lenin, no Stalin, no Mao. No Hitler, no Mussolini. No Ho Chi Minh – no Vietnam War. No H-bomb, maybe.

—He was a Jew, said a boy's voice.

It was Roy, staring me down with a big frown. I hurt too much to be cowed.

—Marx? Was his mother a Jew? His grandmother? I've never heard that, but even if he was, if one snowflake will set off an avalanche, you stop it from falling.

—So righteous, he snapped, all of you. Playing God.

Teacher looked up from his things and told us all to settle down. This was Biology, not History or Ethics. Leave that stuff for when we're in college – or senior Philosophy, if we took that as an elective.

I wasn't sure I held with Evolution, at least not how they were teaching it. If Gott wanted to create new things out of old things, who said he couldn't? Whoever said Creation was over? Time didn't stop after the seventh day any more than it would this week. Vati never said whether or not I should believe whether Gott did or did not exist, but that I should do right or wrong whether or not he did.

Teacher talked about how humans had all come from Africa and that we'd changed in new environments as we wandered across Europe and Asia.

Vati had said the wandering of our people never ended – »Look how far we've come!« – but wherever we are, we have to be true to ourselves. The responsibility for our lives, for our family, to do good and fight evil lies in our hands. »In *your* hands. Who else is going to do it for you?«

Izabel raised her hand and asked,

—Are white people more evolved than black people?

—Are Jews even human, Roy asked back, or are they parasites that evolved to look like the White Man? To blend in?

Bang! – Teacher hit his desk with the textbook he was holding.

—I will not have that kind of talk in my classroom ¶! Roy, one more antisemitic word, and you'll be explaining it to the Principal ¶. Izabel, you're confusing *Evolution* with *progress*. Evolution is biological change in response to changing selective pressures. Were the dwarf elephants we talked about *more* evolved than the larger elephants they evolved from? What does that mean? Have they changed? Yes? Are they *better* elephants, objectively? They were better at surviving on small islands, but on the mainland, they'd be easier prey for large predators like lions and wolves ¶. We don't know why fair skin evolved; only that it did. Nor do we know anything about the complexion of the Neanderthals who were already living in Europe when homo sapiens got there.

Roy raised his hand. Teacher's *yes* was wary. Roy said,

—So, based on what *you* said, would you call fair skin and blue eyes mutations?

—For now, Teacher said, that would be a fair assumption. Pardon the pun.

—And if all humans come from Africa, would you agree that the Negro is the original human?

Teacher crossed his arms, one hinging out to point at need.

—Well, there were other humans besides us in the world, as I've shown you from the fossils. But when it comes to homo sapiens, we can't say for sure what they looked like when they migrated a hundred thousand years ago ¶. If you're specifically talking about the Bantu peoples, there are other ethnic groups native to Africa, like the Bushmen. Who's to say who evolved from whom or who was first? Now, in terms of population, the Bantu are the most successful, so I'll say it isn't unlikely, but it could also be some ethnicity that no longer exists and was outcompeted by them.
—»The most successful«. Thank you.

Teacher didn't sigh, but it was in the droop of his bushy eyebrows. A bridge collapse. Izabel looked like she smelled something bad but didn't raise her hand to complain.

Evolution, as Teacher would have it, went on.

After class, Izabel took my arm on the way to our lockers.
—Can you believe that nigger? she hissed. No wonder no one likes 'em. I wish it wasn't a mixed school. I wish things were like they were before all this about rights.
—Maybe it's better to know what they're thinking.
—I don't wanna know.

I'd be happier if I'd never heard Roy's speechifying, but maybe somebody had to. I put my books away and shut my locker.
—We don't want another Shoah, do we?
—We're not gonna be hiding like Anne Frank. Not from the darkies.
—There's more of them than us.
—Than Jews, sure, but who's gonna go along with it now?
—The Soviets? They hate Jews, too.
—Them and the darkies? I'll believe *that* when I see it ¶. Not taking any books to your next class? she asked. You have Gym?
—I'm going to the nurse's office. I think I need to go home.
—But if your mother can't get you, they won't let you leave.
—I don't know what else to do, I said, hiding a fresh pad under my arm.

I went to the restroom first. I just sat there, letting it drain out of me. Igitt, I didn't want to see.

The nurse said what Izabel said, but at least she let me

lie down. There was no point in calling Mutti. She couldn't leave until school was out, and by the time Vati got here from Downtown, it would be. I was on my own.
—Going back to class? Nurse asked when I got up. I'll give you a hall pass.
—Yes, I lied. I'll try. It's only a few more hours.

I would hall-pass my way back to my locker and then out the door. I stopped in the hall outside the library entrance; I'd seen the Art class paintings on display there before. After what he'd said, the queer one had to be Roy's unless it was by one of his listeners.

It was like some of the stuffy paintings I'd seen of Ancient Rome, but in it, everyone was coloured, and their robes were bright yellows, blues, and greens. Greek-style buildings weren't white stone but yellowy ochre and mixed with little pyramids: narrow ones like teepees. I looked for the signature till I found *Ra* – not initialled RA, but like the Egyptian sun god, Ra. He didn't think too highly of himself, did he?

Roy was hateful, but I couldn't be sure he was up to no good. Vati said I should watch the news, but it was nothing but a bunch of people being angry at each other. Hating, like Roy. Like the coloureds who wore black like the blackshirts in Italy, hating Jews. Were they really connected to the Soviets? Who knew?

It kept starting over. And Roy wore brown, like in Austria. Like in Germany. Maybe he had grey dreams, or maybe he was like everybody else, hating all on his own.

I didn't want to hear Roy any more than Izabel. That didn't mean I could ignore him. The gas chambers, the ovens, the mass graves; it was all on the other side of the hate, whether it was new hate or old.

There was nobody at the lockers. I got my coat and rucksack and wrote a note to Izabel, folded it, and slipped it into hers. I didn't need her mad at me too. I went out a side door and didn't need my hall pass at all, but a lot of kids were out early for the holidays.

Outside, it looked deserted, and the train was empty. Then I almost missed my subway stop, kind of woozy, kind of seasick, though it was on rails.

I froze on the sidewalk across from the house: Mutti's car

was in front. Was she home early for some reason? I didn't know her schedule exactly. It was too late to call, and she was going to yell at me, but what else could I do but go in? I was lightheaded.

Maybe if I was quiet, I could get to my room and lie low. Pretend to come in on time. Maybe.

I unlocked the front door real slow – wincing at the *click!* – before opening it a crack. I peeked in but didn't see anything between me and the stairs. Nobody was in the living room, and the TV was off. I got the door closed behind me, but when I got to the stairs, I could hear them: Oma and Mutti, arguing? I climbed a few steps, the same way I came down in the mornings, till I heard my name:

Ellie is a good girl.

A tree knows when its fruit is rotten, Mutti said. She has »pin-up girls« on her wall, like the greasy men at the auto garage!

She's like that scandalous one that ran off to Berlin, Oma replied. His cousin Bette. The Bohemian. God knows what the Nazis did with her and her kind.

Mutti said, There's something rotten in the blood on Father's side ¶. She's fifteen! And no sign other than she's...

She used a word I didn't know then or misheard. Muggy? Humid?

Mutti added, No children after her, and she will have no children. There will be no grandchildren, no great-grandchildren. She is the end of us. Why did we come here, Mother? For this? We could have stayed with Father until the end.

There was no strength in my legs. I sat hard, and my rucksack thumped. My head was in my arms when Mutti's hands pulled me up. She didn't say sorry. She didn't explain. She didn't demand anything. I didn't look; I couldn't see when, smelling of booze, she took me to my room and closed the door.

The music had stopped. The silence was so strange I didn't notice it at first. I could almost hear my heart if there was a difference between hearing and feeling. My pillow was wet and cold, but I didn't move. Cramps were nothing. Like she'd said, life's not that easy.

A knock came after the light changed. Vati, I thought, but it was Oma asking if I wanted a little something to eat. I asked her to come in and close the door.

She turned my desk chair and sat very properly, very straight, like Herr Klossner wanted me to sit at the piano. Not sad, but resigned, maybe. Dignified in her losses. Always dignified in a way Mutti was not, but Oma wasn't always *here* when she talked to me. Her eyes were distant, seeing beyond the room. The ghosts of the War.

Oma, I said. What did she mean by »Schwule«?

You are old enough to know these things. A »Schwule Mädchen« is a girl who goes with girls.

But I don't, I said. Why would you think… ?

Sara was too afraid for herself to tell anybody. Too scared to see me.

Oma said, I knew your cousin Bette in Stuttgart before she ran off to live her Bohemian life. Who knows if she went to the gas chambers or if they just shot her? I knew her for many years, and I see her in you. She didn't hate men; they meant nothing to her. How long till you run away, Ellie? I know you must.

I'm not, I said. I'm not…

God knows why. The daughters of your father's friends do this too, she said, waving at my clippings. Elvis, the Beetles, the other men little girls fancy and dream of until they are older and find real men like your father.

I didn't mean it like that, I said.

I hadn't. I hadn't known that it could mean that.

She didn't correct me. She didn't argue.

Don't forget me when you go, she said. A »Schwule Weib« will not be able to live only on the piano. I'll bring you a plate.

I didn't correct her. I didn't argue.

»Schwule Mädchen«. A *warm* girl was a funny way to put it. Was that Sara's »little dike« too? Well, I wasn't. Maybe I'd done something wrong. Maybe I'd made a mistake. But it wasn't *me*.

After Oma shut the door, I pulled the pictures down and put them in the wastebasket.

★

C · P · SERRET, PLAYING GOD, VII.

There was a break in the snow. Hanukkah was over, and I had one chance to go to the pictures with Izabel before school next week. The Sixties were over, too, but there was a gap before 1970 started for real.

We'd flown to visit Bubbe and Zayde. They didn't have a piano, so I couldn't play for them. And we'd had visitors of our own: people Vati and Mutti knew. And I could only practise before or after 'cause I had to be there though I wasn't supposed to say anything unless they brought kids my age or mind the younger ones if they were younger. I'd been able to visit Izabel a couple times during Hanukkah, but a lot was going on, and I couldn't take her away for half the day.

Sara didn't call, and when I saw her, she wasn't herself. Smoking cigarettes and saying nothing at all, unreached by Amadio, with his easy movie star grace, or the flood of her aunts, uncles, and cousins. I was so snarled up my mouth was sewn shut, and I couldn't meet her eyes.

And Prokofiev's blue and grey clouds lost their colour; there was only the lashing storm and sorrowed trees and no sign of sun for tomorrow, only the drip, drip, dripping of the leaves. I didn't cry anymore, even though she wouldn't let me say it was a mistake. I'm not one of *those*, no matter what they think.

For the Christmas Concert at school, they'd given me the stage for *Hummelflug*. It was short, but it was something. Polite applause except for Izabel, who reminded me I was her one-and-only piano star.

She was becoming more *Sara* than Sara every day. In eighth-grade Science, the teacher said the moon was getting father and father away, little by little, and one day, it would fly away. That was Izabel. It was hard to see her after school with this or that boy taking up her time. Going here or there for this or that. All December, they'd walked her home most days, not me. Names like *Bradley* and *Chadwick*.

It was never the same boy twice in a row, and I'd hear all about it the next morning. I asked her why no Jewish boys, and she said it wasn't time for Mr Right. Don't look for big fish in a small pond; it would be easier to find her Jewish doctor in college.

The Brads and Chads even got her Westerns, but she'd saved one for me. I was bowled over when I found out it didn't have Clint Eastwood – there went my theory. What was it all about, then?

Once Upon a Time in the West wasn't playing in the Village, so we had to go Downtown.

—You put on makeup? I said.

—Well, we're on a date, aren't we? Just you and me.

—I guess it is, I said, laughing. I've been looking forward to this for two whole weeks!

The teasing was too much like Sara, but I didn't mind. It was kind of sweet that Izabel did all that for me, and she gave me a touch of lipstick on the subway train.

When the picture started, it turned out to be a bunch of sweaty old men! I didn't want to look at that! Nothing was happening on screen, but she was riveted.

I rested my head on her shoulder and let the lights flash before my eyes, *Hummelflug* zipping along in my mind. I never understood all the blood and slaughter over such barren land.

She told me the lady in the black dress was a famous Italian actress. I said,

—If you say so.

Izabel laughed, and I hugged her arm, pulling her closer. Then, at the sad part, she held my hand, and it was nice like it used to be, like a year ago, before high school.

I'd drifted off, I guessed, 'cause she was nudging me, her face so close. Her eyes were dark, her lips parted, her warm hand on the side of my neck; it was a simple thing, the easiest thing, for my lips to reach hers like she was the one leaning in.

Her giggle awakened me from the dream, her eyes wide, her lips curling up against mine, smiling. I sat up, looking down at the floor just past her, over our pressed shoulders, under the empty seats behind us, shamed by the scattered faces looking past us in the flickering dark, under the projector's twinkling star.

I couldn't stop them, couldn't cover them without the hand she still held. My sobs like gasps, breathless, seized.

How could I, what was I… ? – it all ran together, but it was too late. I couldn't take it back. Again.

I closed my eyes to make it all go away, but it was inside with the piano. Izabel's breath in my ear, chills shivered down my spine, and *they* stung like they were being pinched inside my bra:

—I said you were missing it. The kiss.

The piano stopped. There was only the soundtrack inside the theatre. My hands were shaking, and Izabel squeezed my right one with hers.

She shushed me and pulled me back to where I'd been. Against her shoulder, I closed my eyes. I wanted it to be over.

When the lights came on, I hurried to dry my face, but she didn't let go of my hand like I would run away. I said,

—My coat.

—Don't worry, she said. It doesn't count.

—Doesn't count?

—As your first kiss.

—O, you're right, I said.

It wasn't, but she didn't know that. I didn't know how many firsts there were or if I'd any left. I tried to hold back more tears with my frown.

—I didn't mean to laugh, she said. I was surprised, is all. I didn't mean to make you cry.

—I was confused.

I *was* confused but couldn't explain. Izabel said,

—You really were asleep, and it was such a great picture!

She let me put my coat on, then took my other hand. She wasn't letting me get away, I guess. That wasn't so bad.

The Square was busier than when we came in, and the snow began to fall again. Big fluffy flakes drifting like parachutes, tourists pointing, snapping photos and Polaroids. Creepy men hanging by the walls would dart out and try to sell things. I don't know how they could; it was too cold and wet and slippery.

We walked by the edge of the sidewalk to skip all that, avoiding eye contact with them and the bums, or they might be hippies hanging around. Who could tell the difference?

A buttoned-up man with a brown briefcase stepped right in front of us, making us stop. His briefcase popped open, and inside, it was hung with watches, switchblades, and candy-bright lighters. His face was unshaven – no businessman.

—You young ladies want to take a little something home to your parents? A Ball Trainmaster for your pops? A fancy Dunhill lighter for your ma or for yourself!

—I don't smoke, I said. I'm fifteen!

—What's you waiting for?

Izabel pulled me away, and we ran through the crowd laughing till we got away, till I almost slipped and fell, though nobody was chasing us on the slick sidewalk. Her cheeks were all red from running in the cold, her teeth flashing white. There was nothing better than holding hands with her.

There was no place for *Ondine* just yet, though Herr Klossner admitted it was time. Right now, the bumblebee was dancing.

—All that fake junk, she said. Who'd buy any of that?

—How do you know they're fake?

—If they were real, he wouldn't have 'em.

—What about the knives?

—If they catch you with one of those, you'll wind up in the slam.

—So they're real.

—Real bad. Those types don't sell fake guns, neither.

—Why don't the police stop them? They're right out in the open.

—Because then they wouldn't have anyone else to catch. Whatever it looks like, there's always something else going on, she said.

I couldn't say anything to that, but she wasn't like Sara; she wasn't mad or afraid. She wasn't pushing me away. I don't know how it could happen again, how I could make the same mistake when I reminded myself over and over to keep it straight. To keep it kosher.

Izabel said her mother said I could stay for dinner if it was okay with Mutti. I knew she didn't mind. It was out in the open, what Mutti thought, what they all thought, and she didn't have to pretend. No matter what I said, she didn't believe me, and I couldn't watch *Bewitched* anymore either. Didn't matter that I'd taken the clippings down before she said anything.

Three years, she told me. Three years, then on your way.

Oma was wrong. I wouldn't have to run. It wasn't about the piano or conservatory or performing on stage. Ready or not, I had to go.

Vati went all quietlike. All he cared for were his books, his pipe, and tutoring those little kids. He looked at me through his glasses with narrow, squinty eyes, like I was real far away. Only Oma hadn't changed, but she'd watched and never listened all along.

When we got to Izabel's house, it wasn't crowded with cars like during Hanukkah. Her parents' cars weren't there either, but Sara's red Mustang was. Izabel said her father had bought it for himself, but her mother made him give over the keys. It was a convertible and everything. Like her, I couldn't miss it.

It was silent inside like nobody was home. Then, all at once, we ran into Sara and some girl, all made-up, with white-blonde Marilyn curls, coming out of her room right as we were going into Izabel's. They were laughing uproariously and brushed past us like we weren't there. Where was the quiet, sad Sara sitting in the corner a few days ago? I guess she wasn't thinking about me.

Maybe they'd been necking in Sara's room, all alone in the house. She was like that. It was her, and there was no need for me to be sorry anymore.

Closing the door, Izabel stepped back from me.

—What happened!

—What?

—If looks could kill! You know her?

—Never seen her before in my life.

—She give you the evil eye or something?

Did I look angry? I didn't feel, well, I don't know.

—No, I said. I used Izabel's words: —Surprised, is all.

I lay on her bed and covered my eyes. I needed to calm down. She sat next to me.

—Maybe we should try it again.

—What?

—Kissing.

—What?

Lifting my arm, I looked at her.

—Why?

—Like I said, it doesn't count, but what do I do the first time I kiss a boy? I don't wanna laugh, y'know. That would be the worst. I wanna be okay with it.

I could see Sara with that fake Marylin blonde.

—I get it, but...

—No one will know. It's just us.

—Well, I guess.

She knew, at least, I didn't mean anything by it, and she giggled again the first time, but I was ready. I said,

—You sure about this?

—Sorry, let's try again.

I was tense when her lips held mine, then... *then*, I started to feel warm. Spreading across my face, my chest. She said,

—That was okay, right?

—I think so.

—Let's try it the other way.

She didn't explain, her lips caressing mine, a prickly sensation, deep down, rising up.

—What are you doing! I said.

—French, you know. C'mon.

—Um...

—This is why, she said, spreading her hands. You don't want to do that when it's the real thing, right?

—I guess.

So I let her. It was strange at first, till it became like a harmony, played together. I could hear it, rushing, slowing, rising, till the prickling got hot, the humidity sweltering, and I needed to stop. I was Schwule. I was warm and sticky. I pulled back.

—That's enough, right?

—A little more, she said, squeezing my arm. Or is it bad?

—No, it's fine. You're fine.

—But I don't want to be *fine*, Ellie. I have to be good.

She was firm but cool. Like nothing had happened, but it wasn't cool for me. It *was* me.

—How am I supposed to know? I've never kissed anybody before, either.

—Like on TV: when you know, you know. Tell me when it's good.

O Gott, make her stop. I liked it so much. I should have said no. I don't want to do this.

—It's good, I said. It's good.

—You just wanna quit, don't you? Help me, please! It's like when you practise piano.

—Since when do you like to practise?

Izabel huffed at me.

—One more thing, then, okay?

—What?

—Like in the movies, when she looks up into his eyes, and he looks down into hers, and they've got their arms around each other, know what I mean?

—I'm afraid, I said, facing that.

—Why? I'm not gonna hurt you or nothing.

—I'm short; I can't look down into your eyes.

—That's easy. Sit in my lap, then hold me tight like we're in love.

For a moment, the room was grey. It was like a brazen confession with a bare head. I had a choice. I could say no. I could go home. But I sat on her soft lap and slipped my arms around her, playing out the scene she'd sketched. And then her eyes were the only colour till our eyes closed and the music rose and the dancing was in my skin and in my heart and in every space between and I loved her and I loved her and I loved her.

—That was wonderful, I said.

—Finally! Izabel replied, throwing up her hands. Now, get off. I'll put a record on.

★

C·P·SERRET, PLAYING GOD, VIII.

She dropped me just like that. »We'll see each other at school«, she'd said, but not really. I went alone and came back alone. She'd pushed my face into the mirror – like when they pushed a puppy's nose into its own poo – then she'd walked out. Izabel.

At the lockers, there'd be some hulking letter jackets crowding her, and I could scarcely get my books. They were headless 'cause I couldn't bear to look at her smiling up at them.

Izabel would hold my arm in the hallway now and again like a memory, but she had lunch with them, too, though we had the same lunches this semester. She didn't send me away, exactly, but I would've had to sit with them, and I didn't want to. She understood, I guess, and she'd dissuaded the few that tried to include me.

But it was the seventh grade all over again. Alone in the big junior high building without anybody from my elementary. Nobody bothered me in the library. I ate by myself in the cafeteria, listening to my notes. At least I had a hall pass for the pianos.

I did see *that* Roy in the library, but we didn't have any of the same classes. That was my one relief. Nobody picked on me. Nobody noticed me.

It should've been easier, but it wasn't. There were new dreams, confused, hectic. There were fluorescent lights and white hallways; I was running, running. There was something else there; I couldn't hear it or see it, but it was so close. Like a shadow reaching for my shadow. I ran, and I ran, and there was only one clear thing: there, outside the glass, or was I outside seeing it? The black pillar of cloud, ash in the air finer than snow, the dust of human flesh, not against a colourless sky but blue: all of it in colour. Not then, but now. Not there, but here. Not him, but me. A shoah. A new catastrophe.

My eyes were red so many mornings; some kid I didn't

know asked if he could score some grass. I said I was all out. He taught me some weird handshake, then buzzed off.

I practised *Le Gibet* for over an hour. The War had passed from winter to winter to winter and, between, summers not of bumblebees but of flies. Flies over the fields of bodies. They had their own dance, a frenzy, driven mad by the abundant rot. A ragged paper pack of cigarettes in hand, even the smoke didn't keep them away.

It made me feel like steel when I stepped over them: cold and hard and strong. How many had I thrown down with my rifle? With its shattering percussions? How many had I speared before they'd finally speared me?

I didn't want this war, but it was all I could see. Like I'd gone backwards. It wasn't the *Gaspard de la nuit* I was looking for.

Alone but not the only one, I closed the piano. There were other warm girls and warm women. Run away or sent away or right under my nose. There was nothing about them in the books I'd read or the pictures I'd seen. Nothing on TV. Always hidden, like a big secret everyone knew about but me.

Dinner was almost ready. I put on my coat and purse, and nobody said anything when I left. I was like a boarder.

Like in *Die Verwandlung*, in German class, but I wasn't the big beetle – no, I almost fooled myself into thinking that. No, I was like the bothersome people staying in their house that they had to put up with. I had been for a long time, not just recently. Like they'd told Oma to keep an eye on me and make sure I didn't steal the silver, with that one broken chair in my klavierzimmer.

I walked to the Village, to the string of stores getting busy right before they closed for the night. It was almost seven. I walked through the bookshop, looked in the window of some boutiques after they'd locked the doors and flipped their signs. Then I went into the drugstore on the corner.

—What'll you have, little miss?

I pointed.

—Cigarettes, please. In the paper pack.

—Which one? Camels, Marlboros, or Luckies? he said, pointing. Pall Mall?

—Luckies.

I could use some luck. There was no point in cowboy cigarettes if Izabel wasn't going to meet me in »Marlboro country«, and Camels reminded me of Mutti. I saw a lot of kids at school smoking them outside or at the subway station.

—These for your dad?

—Yes, sir.

—Thirty-five cents.

I took some matchbooks. The Zippos were marked five dollars!

I'd seen how they did it, tearing a little hole in one corner, then tapping a cigarette out. I didn't get the trick and had to pull one, but my fingernails were short, and I smushed the end, trying to get it.

My mouth was dry when I hung it from my lips. My hand shaking – like someone would see me, but they were everywhere. Everybody was doing it.

It was like breathing Sara's vodka into my lungs but dry, warm. Familiar. I guess I'd smoked half of Mutti's cigarettes all along without thinking about it. Out of my nose, it was sharp, like I was going to sneeze but didn't.

I went to the soda shop, but it was a sad place to be without Izabel. Without someone to share the float. Nothing worse than one straw. I couldn't drink half of it and lit another cigarette while they were cleaning up. Was that why people smoked? Because they had no company? Because they were alone even when there were a bunch of people around?

When did Mutti not have a cigarette in her hand or hanging from her mouth? I couldn't remember. I could remember sitting in her lap, but I guess even then, she was all by herself.

It was easy to keep lighting new ones after a few minutes. Outside, the drugstore man saw me smoking after he closed shop, but he didn't say anything. It was usual, I guessed. Kids buying cigarettes for their »dad«. It was getting colder, and I walked to Izabel's house. It was closer, but that wasn't why.

I searched, but it was hard to see till I found a little rock like an M&M. Well, three 'cause it took three tries to hit Sara's window. O, she looked mad and held up one finger to her lips.

She came out without putting on a coat.

—What are you doing?

—I don't know. I had to see you.

—Sabelle is here; what if she sees you?

—I'll… I'll think of something.

—Everyone can see us.

—O, it's dark anyway, and it's just two girls talking.

—You came for the way we talked? A pianist talks with her hands. I remember.

—What about you? I said, my fingertips pressing where she'd left her mark. You're talking about yourself.

—Perhaps. Perhaps I am.

Sara shook her head over crossed arms, a bitter smile.

—You shouldn't have come.

—Don't you understand? I needed to see you.

—There's nothing we *can* do. Don't *you* understand?

—O, take me out, I said. Take me away.

—What excuse do I have to take my sister's friend anywhere without her too? Even if we weren't what we are, if I was a college man, I couldn't. I couldn't, even if some of them do. It's wrong, Ellie. I'll be twenty soon, and you're in high school. A freshman like Sabelle. Can't you see?

—I don't care.

—Then I have to care for both of us. Don't do this again.

—Ellie! What happened! came Izabel's voice from above.

—Nothing, I said.

—Come up!

—Okay.

Sara blanched, and not from the cold.

—See, how will you explain?

—I'll think of something.

—Then, come in. It's too late now.

I followed her into the mess I'd made. Mrs K was a doll.

—Ellie! she said when she saw me. Did something happen at home?

—It's okay, ma'am. I had to get some air.

She lowered her voice:

—Do you need me to call your mother?

—No, please. It'll be alright; I'll go back in a little while.

—We already had dinner, but do you need something to eat? You must be frozen.
—No, thank you, ma'am. I'll visit with Izabel a little bit if that's alright.
Mrs K sent me up, and Sara walked behind me, saying nothing. Izabel was waiting by her open doorway, and the look that passed between them was hot, like a flash of lightning.
—What were you two doing? she said, closing the door.
—It's a secret.
—From me? She's my sister, not yours.
—Well, it's about your birthday. Don't spoil it.
—My birthday, right, silly me.
She said it like she knew I was lying, thought it was funny that I'd tried to lie, and she wanted me to know.
—Come here, she said, patting the bed beside her. I need your help with something.
—Anything, I said to get away from Sara.
—You remember before, when we practised? Y'know.
—Um, yeah.
—I need you to do it again, but not all soft and cosy like before. Harder. Pushy, like a boy would do it.
—Izabel, I can't, I said. Don't make me.
—It's the last time, she said. Please? Only you can help me. I don't want to ask one of the other girls.
Like a slap in the face, I could see it. Some other girl's mouth touching hers, and I wouldn't have it. I wouldn't. I wanted to say, I love you, I love you, don't make me do it, but I said,
—Alright. One last time, promise?
—Promise!
She laid back on her pillow and beckoned me closer. The fear came back. I said,
—Like that?
—Get on top.
Her smile was so strange, her eyes so dark, like in the movie house. She pulled me to her, against her; I was sinking, drowning; it was too much, but she held me tighter, and my heart was going so fast and it was so hot I needed to open

the window and I wanted her to stop but she wouldn't let me speak; so I'd make her stop, I'd give her the pianist's hands that Sara didn't want and she would make me go away like Mutti and never see me again but at least it would be over.

But she didn't.

Izabel didn't stop me, and I became the spring storm that Sara sheltered from, raining over Izabel with my hands and my mouth and pressing my softness into hers like the gathering of clouds till I didn't know what else to do. Till I'd reached the end of myself: I wouldn't do *that* and pushed away hard till she let me free.

I looked at my empty hands. Mein Gott, they burned like needles had stabbed into my palms, but betweeen them, a crime. Her open blouse, her lacy bra with its little blue bow up to her throat. If I'd worn lipstick, it would have looked like murder.

Her mussed skirt. I remembered the rough drawing, but I hadn't. Not all the way. *That* was real, but this wasn't real to her. She was going to fly and take this away.

—I get it now, she said. That's what he wanted.

Her eyes were far away. She'd been thinking about someone else. Not my hands, but his – whichever *him* it was, the bloom of pink across her fair skin wasn't for me. I hadn't lost. I'd never had a chance.

—You didn't let him, I said.

—No, I freaked out. I mean, I knew, but I wasn't ready when he tried. But I get it now. I should be okay next time.

I dropped my hands. There was no surrender, then. Just shoot.

—How can we be friends like this?

—Because you love me.

I stared at her.

Izabel said it again; then I whispered,

—What?

—You love me.

A third time. I'd really heard it. She said,

—Your mother called Maman, and she told me all about it. You're like those boys who are light in the loafers. She says artists are like that sometimes. I told her you're a sweetie pie and never once tried to do anything bad. Whatever your

mother said, you were a good girl – except something happened between you and Sari that Maman doesn't know about ¶. You two were talking too loud outside. Maman could have heard ¶. She doesn't know you were pretending to be sweet and innocent. That you were just waiting to get your hands on me all this time. I wish I had a Polaroid of your hickie, but I didn't have it yet.
—You saw it!
—Silly, of course, I saw it. I couldn't miss Sari's lipstick all over your face! I just didn't say nothing. I would've told Maman, but I didn't wanna get you in trouble, and when she told me about you, I knew you loved me. You were in love with me the whole time, weren't you? Always looking at me with those big, sad eyes. You remember in seventh grade? You never said anything, but it's like you were trying to paint my picture.
She laughed.
—That's right. All junior high, the boys *were* looking at you, Miss Hepburn, but you were looking at *me*. It was me, not Sari, but she gave you some grass or something, didn't she? She thinks she's so smart like the rest of us don't have noses ¶. It all makes sense now: you thought I wouldn't let you, so you tried to go back to her. You can forget about her now.
The Earth disappeared from under me. I was out there, in the dark.
—When did you know? When did my mother call?
—O, it was a while back. Before Hanukkah – before your hickie faded. I need to show you how to cover those up, by the way. Everyone kept asking me about it.
—O God.
—It's fine, Elle. You're a regular girl, and no one knows any better. But I know you wanted me like that, loved me like that all along.
It sank in; the timing. I said,
—Then in the movie house that day?
—I was curious. I wanted to see what you'd do if I gave you a chance. Only I laughed like a dum dum.
It was in her eyes like I was seeing them for the first time. She wasn't my »hanger-on«; I was hers from the beginning.

Izabel was gifted, they said. She had to know everything, even if she didn't show off in front of people. Izabel had to be perfect, effortlessly perfect like I'd used to think. Like she'd made it look, but now she didn't even cover herself.

—But you've helped so much, and there's a little more you can help me with tonight.

—But you don't want me, I said, choking up.

—What's that matter?

Was it shame? Was it anger? This pain in my heart?

—I think I'm ready, she said, lifting her skirt. I heard some other things boys like to do. What else do you know?

★

C · P · SERRET,
PLAYING GOD, IX.

I thought she'd used me up. The taste of her in my mouth, I washed her from my fingers, from my face. I thought it was over, but once I'd seen the real her, once I'd seen her anguished frown, only the promises were over.

Not even two weeks later, she started walking me home again, not every day, but she'd come up to my room and turn the radio on. One of her stations. For *that* again. Her favourite thing the boys couldn't do right or didn't care to. »Broute mon gazon,« she'd say in my ear at school, smiling. *Graze on my grass*, but only when it was risky – surrounded by the school crowd and the din of a thousand voices.

No matter how much I wanted her to, she never touched me except to pull my hair. I was *Elle* again, now that she had me by it, and she was my *Belle*. I started pinning it up, and she took a tighter hold. She said,

—You love me, and I let you. You were my first, and you've had more than any boy, but you *know* you have to take care of yourself. Any of them would kill to take your place.

I got so mad, but it ended up worse when she wanted to see – when she had to know. She and her camera.

The worst was I was afraid she'd stop letting me. So I was always afraid. That she might want a Polaroid of something else. That she might not want anything at all. I knew how warm she got down there, the fever inside, and I craved her worse than cigarettes. *They* ate up all my weekly pocket money, and I had to ask Vati for more.

I had a whole story prepared, but he started giving me tens instead without looking at me. It hurt that it was that easy. Like he was paying me to stay away.

That's how February became March, right up to the Easter holiday, then nothing all that week off from school. My sunless spring. »You love me«, a hex, and I was lost.

Gaspard de la nuit was a Labyrinth, and there was no way out. The Minotaur wouldn't let me leave, but I was afraid it might make me. Herr Klossner listened, nodding here and there as his cigarette burned back like an incense stick.

I see »die Passion«, he said, but I know this is not what you see. The Passion is a great suffering. The greatest sacrifice. Forgiveness for the sinners. Forgiveness even for those who lash us, crown us with mocking thorns, who crucify us with nails and, when we cannot resist, lance us with their spears ¶. Forgive me for speaking of Christian things, Gentile things, but this is the genius of which I have spoken. This is not an inhuman terror, and you have communicated what we have all known in our own ways. We suffer and die. We are tormented and killed. But do we die with hate in our hearts? It is a question and perhaps not the place of a German to say such things to Jews, he said, bowing to Oma.

She nodded stiffly once.

The Labyrinth terrified me, but it held me to Izabel. Who could I forgive? My *Gaspard de la nuit* didn't have an answer that I could hear or see. Only the long shadows and the hollow places, something, *something* always waiting, always ready. Maybe it was me. Could I be forgiven? Who could do such a thing?

He asked me if I was satisfied.

I said, No, I'll keep working.

Then, *Scarbo*, he prompted me.

I'd heard Argerich, a real Wunderkind, on the radio. She was Sara's age, they said. I was nowhere near her, lost in Izabel's Labyrinth.

There were no letter jackets around when Izabel pinched the flesh of my arm and twisted so hard I almost screamed aloud. She pressed me to the lockers.

—Elle, did you think I wouldn't notice you staring at that girl right in front of me?

—What girl? No, I wasn't, ow... oww... !

She twisted again, and I held it in, mostly.

—Belle, please, I said. Ple-ase, there's only you. Please.

—I'll believe you, but don't let those eyes stray again. She rubbed the sore spot on my arm, saying, —I was thinking, don't go to a conservatory. Take music at the college I go to, then we can share a dorm room. You'd love that, wouldn't you?

My face got hot, and I hated my transparent skin. And a

cold lump, like an ice cube, stuck in my throat that I couldn't swallow, but it tickled me *there* all the same. Izabel's braced smile glinted, almost vicious, like knives. My protest,

—But my music!

—My piano star doesn't need a conservatory. I'll help you with your grades and SATs; I'll take care of everything ¶. You wanted us to live together, right? So why wait ¶? They're waiting for me. I'll see you after lunch.

She made a little kissy face that nobody else could see, and my heart pounded for it. I was hers, and she wouldn't let me go. She'd burned through her new friends, and the cheerleaders didn't take to her like the boys' JV.

My locker creaked shut, my lunch inside. Izabel had me turned around. For nine days, she hadn't let me – all of the Easter holiday week and this one. Now this?

I'd end up a piano teacher, living near her and her Jewish doctor husband and their kids. Probably teaching them piano too. I'd be there for her whenever she needed unless she could replace me, and who would get trapped in her Labyrinth like I had?

I folded my third-full pack of Luckies and tucked it up my sleeve, and I passed through the library on my way out. No luck yet, but it was a good shady spot to sit and be by myself, and the upperclassmen hanging out down in the trees, smoking, necking, or whatever they were doing didn't bother me.

A white handkerchief was the warning, folded up near the exit. It was monogrammed, *Ra*, again.What was it that Roy had said about playing God? I balled it up like Kleenex. I'd find something dirty to clean with it.

They were out there like before, but there were more of them. Six, no, seven. I stopped in the strip of shade and lit a cigarette. *Jews this*, *Jews that*. Roy was exactly the same. Up to no good.

One of them pointed me out real quick. Roy didn't look surprised at all.

—I was going to paint you a picture, but *here* is the soldier of Zion.

—You have no idea who I am, I said, joining the coloureds along the wall.

I sat by the stairwell, next to the two who were smoking. Roy appeared more at ease than before.

—Not all of you know that I love to paint and that my parents supported me becoming a painter. I could have gone to the Arts high school, but I came here. Why? Because I have a higher calling. You have a higher calling. We can't always do as we wish when there is a greater need, and the need has never been greater ¶. How will the Negro find his worth in a nation that does not belong to him? In a land where he is less than, where the new men rule over the ancient men. The true men.

He held up three fingers.

—Science tells us that there is no Eden but Africa. That the White Man is a mutation, and the Jew is a parasite on all peoples ¶. And within this nation, this Republic, the whites and the Jews have all of the power but bear no responsibility. How can that be! Power without accountability?

Roy pointed.

—One man, one vote. One woman, one vote, right? Fair, right ¶? So tell me, when Negroes have no work, who is held accountable? No one is held accountable. When Negroes have no food, who is held accountable? No one is held accountable. When Negroes have no medicine, and we die younger than everyone else, who is held accountable? No one is held accountable ¶. When Greenwood, the Black Wall Street they don't teach us about, was burnt down, the Negroes massacred in the streets, who was held accountable? No one was held accountable.

—Truth, plain truth, a voice.

—Can we envision a Negro democracy whose leadership bears responsibility and is held accountable for its decisions? Look up there. They have billions for the moon and nothing for starving Negro children ¶. We are preparing ourselves to go into the spiritual danger of the Jewish universities. The charnel houses of Marxism...

Under the hazy half-moon in a clear blue sky, it was the same young voice, the same words that were not young.

He was him, but not him. He was probably a good Protestant boy and couldn't believe he was one with his grey dreams and that he'd inherited his will.

The cat is dead. The cat is alive. And so am I.

Roy was far ahead of *him* at the same age. There was no comparison. To stop Roy now, in high school, wouldn't be easy, but tracking him down later would be even harder.

I could lose everything. Unless I gunned him down like Jack Ruby, I could die. Roy was a foot taller than me, and it might not be possible at all. I could die for nothing, but as he spoke, I could smell *that* smoke, feel the grit and ash in my eyes. It all became black and white.

Roy was saying,

—Like our very own Zionist, here, the Marxist is no respecter of borders or homeland. What is the East European now but another Russian? Who are the Panthers under Brezhnev ¶? We can learn a lesson from the Jews. Yes, I said it: we can learn a lesson from the Jews. What other race has preserved itself and maintained its separateness better than the Jews? Five thousand years, six thousand!

Roy pointed to me.

—But racial solidarity is not enough. It's not enough for us to live in the ghettos of white cities. We must have the will to win our freedom and build our independence ¶. The early men who left Africa were Negroes. He jabbed his finger at the school, saying, —They know the White Man is a bastard race. They know the White Man mixed with Neanderthals and God-knows-what-else that they keep buried. You notice they never call the Negro a »Cave Man«. They never paint a picture of a Cave Man who's black.

—You know that's right, a voice.

—The Negros who remained in the Motherland are pure. The true humans. The strength of body and minds that built the Nubian pyramids, that birthed all civilisation, is the same strength that built this nation. They stood back and watched as we built it, then claimed the fruits of our labours. Whether by secession or revolution, the White Man will let my people go.

—Yes! other voices.

I stubbed out my cigarette.

—And what will you do when your ideal state is full?

—Expand. We were the first people, and we will reclaim what is ours.

—By conquest? Ein tausendjähriges Reich?

He raised his chin.

—Our Judenrein will be everlasting. A pure Negro state from sea to shining sea. Noch irgendwelche Fragen, Jüdlein?

—Nein. Ich verstehe dich sehr gut.

No. No more questions. There was no room for doubt.

»Judenrein«. A place cleansed of Jews.

It was all ash, all darkness. No future. Not Izabel's. Not mine. I thanked »Herr Arnold« for his enlightening talk and went back inside. I'd had enough.

I still had his stupid handkerchief and, till I needed a napkin or to shine my shoes, I put it in my locker on my way to the auditorium. It was usually empty unless there was a Drama class. I didn't have much time, but a few minutes of slow practise would soothe my mind.

—You were so hard to find! Izabel called almost as soon as I'd started. I checked the music room first. Come here, she said, pulling me from the bench and off-stage into the wing.

—What's going on? I asked.

She kissed me, and I melted in her arms. The dike burst, exploding, gushing; my limbs detached, floating away.

I'd needed it; I needed it so bad after all this time. For her to hold me close, to lift and squeeze me to her, to take my breath away till only one foot touched the ground.

Her voice was extra breathy:

—I can be super-nice, baby, from now on; I can kiss you the way you like. Before you get your face all wet, anyway.

We were still in the auditorium, and someone might see, but Izabel kissed me. We were going to be late for the next period, but she kissed me, my back to the wall. Class cut.

—You love it, she said, squeezing my Möpse. You love me.

She kissed me till I said yes to everything. Till I confessed that I loved her minou, amını – all the dirty words she'd taught me – till I didn't know what I was saying. Till I would've set fire to the concert grand. I was quivering.

—And after school, she said after sucking my lower lip, I'll make it extra special. I'll let you rub yourself against me, y'know, like this.

I'd thought of it, I'd imagined it – I'd tried it with my pillow – but I'd never have said it to her and her camera. I said,

—Curious?

She'd seen all of me. My anguish face. She'd left nothing private.

—It's only fair, baby, she said. I wanna take care of you too.

Take care of me by letting me push away on top of her like the boys did. Then, *then*, it shocked me like one of her pinches, and my mouth dropped open. *Baby*.

I was right. I was going to be her wife. Her second spouse, off-stage, waiting on her hand and foot, out of sight. She'd proposed, and I'd kneeled and begged, »I do! I do!«

»After school« was our wedding night. Our April honeymoon. Like they said on TV, we would seal the deal.

That was her answer to my *Gaspard de la nuit*. There was no door, no way out. I was sealed in forever. A ring, not of gold but of stone. I said,

—I won't be able to think of anything else the rest of the day.

I wasn't lying. Izabel smiled her silvered devil smile, her winner's smile, and gave me a tiny little peck on the mouth. Not a promise but a bargain. She'd let me get her a little dirty for the low, low price of my soul.

There was time before the class after the one we'd cut, so she put my hand down there for »a quick one«, she said, but even that wasn't enough. Holding my wrist, Izabel put my wet fingers into my mouth.

The way she stared: her funny little open-mouth smile. The more I savoured her, the more she liked it, but not enough to choose me. Not enough to try. At least she didn't have her bag. No camera.

But it was queer and kinda put the zap on my head. Why now? Why already? How could she be so sure? Three years till graduation, and she was planning our sleeping arrangements in a school we hadn't applied to yet. It nagged me through the long anticipation – after I'd signed on her dotted line.

Nine days. I'd counted them, afraid Izabel had dropped me for good this time, afraid she hadn't. What could have happened in nine days?

What's going on? What *was* going on? – that wasn't necking.

Then, *then*, she corrected me. In my room, my chair under

the doorknob, she corrected me, guided me, and she was right.

The low after was lower than the high was high. Before I could catch my breath, I had to say it:

—You did it with somebody else!

It wasn't for me; it was for her. She already knew she liked it that way and had to teach it to me herself. Someone from school – no, somebody older, somebody more experienced. A college girl? A teacher?

—Don't be that way, baby. I didn't mean anything by it; I just needed to know if it was different with someone else.

—But if you like it so much, why can't it be the two of us?

—I told you, I'm no broute-gazon. I liked that she liked me, but I love how you love me. No one else loves me the way you do.

Broute-gazon. Me. The other girl. *Grass-grazers*. She was never going to choose me over anybody. More like she was keeping me in her purse. She'd pull me out like a cigarette and burn me up.

—I can't anymore, Belle, I said. Not like this.

Izabel let me stew, but I could see it. I could see her calculating.

—Will you always be there for me? Always and forever?

—Yes! Yes... !

—Then, I'll be your one and only, and I won't need anyone but you.

Except for her boys, she meant. They came first. And when the time came, it would be her husband, her family. And other men. Would she really give them up after the ring? I couldn't see it. I said,

—What else did you learn?

—O, we'll talk about *that* next time.

Her smile said everything, but she squeezed me and cuddled me to turn my frown upside down, and it worked. But we couldn't stay like that for long – Mutti's reserve had its limit. Izabel told me to walk her home, but I pretended to say no, and she wouldn't let up till I said yes like I was going to. I needed the walk back to think it over alone. Cigarette after cigarette.

Grey ashes hung in the air, and not from my Luckies. I had to do it. The black cloud was there even at night.

Izabel wasn't going to give me two days in a row, so the next day, I took the subway Downtown after school. Down to the Square, looking for a familiar face, and I found him, less buttoned up, still not quite clean-shaven. A different briefcase, but the same harrowed look like a stray dog.

He didn't notice me till I lit another cigarette, the sound of the match igniting beside him.

—What's doing, little lady? You can't be using cheap paper matches! Let me show you some nice lighters...

I let him run a few by me till I picked out a knife instead. There were a few sizes, and I chose the biggest one.

A shiny black handle with a metal button in the middle and little silver hooks on the open end, facing clockwise like a swastika. It snapped open just fine, but he had to show me where to press to close it. The blade was shaped like a bayonet's.

—Do you have any guns? I asked him.

—Guns? he said, grinning. Whaddya take me for? I ain't no criminal.

He leant closer and nodded *that* way. There were alleys here and there between the tall buildings, but he lowered his voice:

—They's places where you can find tings like dat, but – pretty girl like you – is more likes to get got than to get, if you know what I mean.

He straightened.

—Is your old man... ?

—No. Nothing like that. I'll take it.

It was nice for a stranger to give a crap. I wrapped it in Roy's handkerchief and put it in my rucksack.

At home, Oma was busy in the kitchen, and I looked in before going up. A brisket, probably for tomorrow. I asked if she needed help. She said, The pianist help with dinner? What would you know how to do?

I told her, Well, okay, I wondered if you could cut my hair before we eat? Like to here.

You could say this in the first place and save everyone time. Let me find the scissors upstairs. Sit there.

I had to be quick. I took a deep breath before the large mound of skinned red flesh.

The first stab only pricked it with the tip. The second, halfway. It wasn't hard, but I had to hit it like I meant it. Like it was whatever girl had touched Izabel, then the point hit the wood underneath. Whoever she was, she'd changed Izabel's mind about kissing, about touching my Möpse and Hintern. She must've liked it so much I couldn't stand it.

It's how she was. If Izabel could get more from anybody, she'd take it. It wouldn't stop. The other girl must have dumped her: *that* was all the urgency. That's why she put the leash on my dog collar. Nine days? Nine-and-a-half till right now.

The other girl. The other woman. I didn't hate Roy; I was terrified of what he'd become. Her, I hated.

Izabel had almost wrecked my best bra getting it off me yesterday, and then, what was that? Who was that? And I didn't even know who she'd been thinking about. Me or her. It was so good, and it was *the worst*. I wanted to stab the brisket again.

I checked the tip of the blade quick: I didn't want to bend it before I had to use it for real. I wiped it with the edge of the tablecloth and dropped it in my bag. I'd wash it upstairs when nobody was looking. I sat and waited for Oma.

Izabel was selling me a song. How often would I see her with all the college boys around? No, it wasn't a song but a dream. It wasn't even my dream. Someday, when I'm alone in our dorm, waiting for her to come back from one of them, I'll jump from the roof of her damned college.

I fetched out my cigarettes. I'd forgotten how to wait.

Like in my grey dreams, I didn't want this war. I didn't, and I'd lost the piano fighting it before. I'd lost it, my fingers, my life, but if I hadn't fought it, if nobody had stopped them, it would've been worse. The sky of the whole world would have been blackened with smoke, everything dusted with the ashes of the dead. The disposed.

This was my life – my only life, but after those dreams, it felt like a second chance. But what did I really have to lose? I wasn't a big fish in a small pond – I didn't have a pond at all. This was a fishbowl. I was a fish they fed but not much else.

I wasn't Argerich – someone who'd been on stage since she

was eight. I guess it wasn't fair: I only had the piano, but one thing that mattered still counted as a sacrifice. That's what they used the Labyrinth for, didn't they? For sacrifices?

Even if it meant the gibbet, I had to try. Roy was making long-term plans, strategic plans, and gathering followers. What could I do against him? Me, a short girl who played piano and couldn't help with dinner? Surprise, maybe?

Maybe like Pearl Harbor. He couldn't see it coming.

★

C·P·SERRET/ PLAYING GOD/ X.

We bought challah from a Village bakery for the weekends. Vati said Oma shouldn't »potchke« in the kitchen. The bakery bread was better than hers, but we'd never say that. Maybe she knew and didn't say either. She would take a small piece but didn't eat it.

The doorbell rang.

I'll get it, I said, rising.

No, finish that, Oma said. You need to eat at least one meal a week.

—Pardon me, I'm very early, Sara said, following Oma back in.

Sara was always beside me. I can't imagine what it would be like if she was still in high school. Probably walking me from class to class.

—Look at that pannim, Vati said, Ellie is always so glad to see you. We appreciate you helping to take care of her with your great loss. Really, she should be helping you.

Mutti gave him a look, and he stopped. I stuffed one cheek like a squirrel and excused myself. She didn't ask where we were going so early before my music lesson. It was Sunday. What wouldn't stay closed all day wouldn't open till later. I didn't know either: I wanted to leave, and that's what they wanted too.

—Where are we going? I asked Sara in the living room.

—Can we talk in your room?

—No, we should go.

—Very well.

The pillar of cloud was there and not there. Roy was stopped, and he wasn't. Behind bars, for now. It wasn't a question of life or death but whether the cage would open now or later. Whether his voice would pass through those bars like sparks and flames would spread after all.

When we were in her car, she looked me over before starting the engine.

—Is it *that* bad?

—They've already evicted me, I said. Three-year notice.
—They know?
—They never asked me; they never believed me when I said no. Everybody knows.
—That's… I'll think of something.
I appreciated her saying that, but who knew what would happen when my day of atonement came. When Mrs K found it. When she showed Mutti. If they showed it to Sara.
We drove through midtown, the usual route she took to the South Side. She was so quiet I got nervous and lit a cigarette.
—Give me one, she said.
I gave her mine and lit another. I guess she was nervous too.
—The deposition, she said. What did the DA say?
—You could've called.
—No, I need to hear it in person.
—I didn't see him, but the ADA says the case probably won't come to trial till early next year. They're still investigating, but they've tied him to two other cases in the City. I shrugged, saying, —Similar weapon; witnesses saw a tall coloured man. »The same lack of hesitation«, he said, but I don't know how they would know that.
—I do, she said. I've seen dead bodies, real ones, in anatomy class. They say when someone does that for the first time, they hold back at first. It's why the news says nasty things like »stabbed seven times.« Things like that. A good person doesn't want to hurt anyone, and even when they lose control, they have to work up to it. Can't quite do it at first ¶. I thought… I thought, »He's done it before.« One stab, like an assassin, after he tried to rape her. They say he didn't, but how can they…
Her lips were pressed tight, and the last few words barely passed between them, her knuckles white on the steering wheel. In a hurry, I said,
—The ADA also said they've got a bunch of witnesses, teachers and students from Latin, ready to testify about Roy making antisemitic comments in class. They're gonna move to get him tried as an adult. With three murders and the other stuff, he said it should be »a slam dunk« ¶. But he said

the death penalty can't be used against juveniles, even if he's tried as an adult. State law.

—If they let him out for a single day, I will kill him.

—No, Sara!

Her eyes flashed.

—Don't you want the same?

—Yes, but let me put him away. Don't...

—He deserves the chair.

—He deserves to be in a dark hole for the next hundred years, looking at the sky through iron bars. But if they do let him out, if he lives long enough to step outside...

I squeezed her arm.

—I'll help you kill him.

I never wanted to hurt anybody, but it was too late to be a »good person«. She squeezed my hand with hers.

—I love you, Ellie.

I was dazzled like the world lit up as bright as a flashlight in my eyes. I'd never heard such a thing.

—Sara, I...

—I mean... she said over me, then blushing, *blushing*, said under her breath: —Ah, mon Dieu.

Sara didn't look at me for a long while, and I couldn't stop looking at her and the theatre of emotions playing across her face while she drove, unable to get away. Had I ever said it? Maybe Vati had asked if I'd loved him sometime back, but maybe I was remembering something from TV. I never told Izabel: it was her line: »You love me.«

—Are you going to hold me forever? she said.

—Yes, I think so.

It wasn't the words I'd only heard on TV, but the way she'd said them. Like the sound hadn't come from her throat or her heart but from deeper down in her belly. Like she'd said something in Turkish, French, or their other language, Ladino, and I didn't know what it meant. But I wanted to.

When we parked near Herr Klossner's, she asked me to go over my deposition word by word. The exact questions, my exact answers. I asked why she'd want to listen to all *that* again. She said she needed to hear every word.

—I needed to be there, but I couldn't.

My testimony was weak. I said I didn't see anything except

Roy leaving with a dark-haired girl. It looked like Izabel, but it couldn't be. He hated Jews, and he hated her. I didn't worry till I couldn't find her before the school conference and went to look where Roy had gone. I only saw the aftermath.

He'd left the school grounds by himself, »fled the scene«, they said, during school hours, and he had no alibi. I never said I saw him do anything. They made up the story. He must have threatened Izabel with the knife, they said. Got her alone with everyone else going to the conference rooms. I didn't give them any theories.

Sara wasn't embarrassed at all when the tears started. She called him a nigger and other ugly words like she was spitting up.

—But her… Why her?

—He hated her from before – everybody saw it in Biology – but he'll come for all of us one day if he can, him and his followers. The Jews, anybody white no matter where they're from, any coloureds that get in his way. He's evil, and more and more people are listening to him. It reminds me of the Thirties, I said.

She frowned at me through her tears as if I'd said something queer. Of course, I wasn't there in the Thirties, but everybody knew. Then she glanced at the Navy watch she could read without her big glasses and said it was almost time.

In his klavierzimmer, Herr Klosser put a new piece on the music desk.

BARCAROLLE
from Troisième *recueil de chants*
Op. 65, No. 6
Charles-Valentin Alkan

What's this? I asked.

Something different, he said. The challenge will be in your feelings, your sensitivity, and in exposing yourself by leaving the notes bare. It is a time of loss and grief. You are young to have seen what you were forced to see, and you could not save your friend ¶. It is not a dirge or some great show of melancholy, for there is joy also in the remembrance of the lost, in our love for them, in the shared joys of living, as much as we mourn our loss. Joy and grief, they go together ¶. Come, read briefly, then begin.

It was short. I could hear it, but I could only see one thing:

If there was a chance, I wrapped it in my raincoat.

—He's going, I said.

—What? Izabel said. Everyone's going.

She was always dragging her feet, keeping me with her at the lockers till the last minute to tease me, pinch me, or say dirty things. The letter jackets didn't hang around anymore, but they let her hang around them. It made her testy. I said,

—Not to the auditorium. Outside. Roy might be up to no good.

—Him? Like what?

—Like Kent State. Once everybody's inside, he could set fire to the building.

That was the whole to-do in the lecture halls and auditoria: the entire school stopped for the teachers to talk to us about the »massacre«. The news was everywhere, and I couldn't get away from it. It's not like Vietnam was over or the Soviets had said *nevermind* and given half of Europe back.

—Tell a teacher! she hissed.

—They're already inside. I'll go have a peek, I said. I'll meet you there.

—No, she said, grabbing my arm. He could be dangerous. Besides, it's raining. Nothing's gonna catch fire.

—It will if he uses gasoline. The teacher's parking lot is back there, behind the library. All the gasoline you could want.

Izabel complained but held my arm. The library was closed, but there was another exit nearby on the south side of the school, around the corner from Roy's stage. I stopped at the turning point and peeked: he was there, alone, the raindrops darkening his light clothes. She was right behind me.

—Cowards, he said clearly. Cowards!

Roy balled his fists and with long, quick strides reached and descended the stairs. I towed Izabel to the corner of the stairwell. I tried to peer down, but the branches obscured the parking lot.

—I don't think he's going that way, she said, and he might see us.

—We'll go through the trees. If he leaves, we'll go right back.

The copse was ringed by the concrete wall and stairs and the asphalt lot, but under the clouds, it was dark. I led her over the low wall and down the slippery slope. The earth under the trees was firm, but the patchy grass was wet and crisscrossed with slick roots. Cigarette stubs were everywhere, pressed in by shallow shoe prints with heel divots.

—Isn't that him there? she said, trying to shield her eyes from the droplets. He's crossing the lot to the street, right? Let's get to the auditorium before we get in trouble.

I stabbed the knife into the side of her neck, and she almost pulled me down, dropping like someone cut the tendons in her legs. After the first gouting red mist, she made a terrible hiccuping, gurgling sound.

No pleading eyes asked why. Izabel didn't look at me: her eyes rolled up, then grimaced closed, until she went silent, and the convulsions stopped. I stood above her, knife raised while the fine rain pitter-pattered on the leaves above us. I wasn't shaking. My heart was steady.

I'd seen Roy with his followers in the hallway. Heard him say,

—Whites killing whites. Every Negro here should meet me outside. I'll tell you what's what. Let them have their conference. We'll have ours.

I'd gotten goosebumps and stayed out of sight. Something wasn't right. I didn't know what I could do, but I'd try.

Her blood looked black, like oil, glistening on the presoaked dirt. I tossed my raincoat back a ways and wiped the knife with Roy's handkerchief over and over till it gleamed; then, I dropped it in the oily patch. At the edge of the lot, I balled up his bloody handkerchief and threw it as hard as I could between the parked cars.

I went back to Izabel, lying there motionless, and with my clean hand, I tore at her blouse, popping buttons. No bloody fingerprints. I flipped her skirt and pulled hard on the hem of her panties till the stitching popped. Just askew was enough.

My right cuff was stained, and the spray got my dress. I tripped myself over an exposed root, bruising my hands and knees; then I crawled to Izabel till I was all cold muck and filth. I left my hand prints on her cheeks, and the rain threaded them with rivulets. I shouldn't have, but I risked getting blood on my face and kissed her goodbye, the raindrops falling heavier. *Thud, thud. Thud, thud.* Black rain stained with ash.

Then, back up the stairs and around the corner to the side doors, I took a deep breath and started screaming before I pulled one open.

It didn't catch up to me till I was sitting in the Principal's office while they shouted at each other just outside, waiting for the police. It stole in like a shadow I'd left behind, but I could never escape it. It would never leave me, never let me go. I cried like I'd never cried before, and the police had to answer their own questions.

They never found the handkerchief, but it didn't matter. I'd killed the white bird and hung it from Roy's neck, and the stain of her blood had passed from me to him. I looked at Sara looking at me. Like the sky, her eyes didn't blink.

Herr Klossner said, You have not been one to elaborate on the score, but here, to expose yourself, you improvised?

I had to.

For what I couldn't unsee or undo, I left unsaid.

He said, It is the first time I showed you this score, I know. Did you hear it before on the radio?

No.

Did you perhaps seek out Oscar Peterson, as I suggested?

No, not yet.

—Such a disconcerting child, Herr Klossner said to Sara. To play such a piece in that way cold.

—Cold?

—It was her first time seeing this music. I thought she might have listened to Jazz on her own.

—It sounded like classical piano.

—It was not Jazz, true, but something missing from many modern pianists: the vision to create from the composer's line. You see the mountains, yes, but there is also the sky. The clouds, the stars, the sun, and even God. It is not, perhaps, for her to play Jazz or Blues but to see the vista beyond what is written and memorised by so many ¶. Once, all musicians could improvise from the composer's lead. It is not for the piano to only be a stagnant machine of reproduction like the radio or record player. To play is not a test of live re-creation. What you heard was a new voice: her voice.

—Hers? A real genius, then.

—She has an impressive teacher, he said and laughed.

Her beauty was getting to his head. I don't know why she sat through my lessons the way Oma had to.

Sara didn't like their lentil soup. »No wonder you're petite,« she'd said, »if that's how they feed you at home.« But instead of dropping me off and picking me up afterwards, she stayed every time and watched me play.

I could feel her eyes along on my neck – like a caress sometimes. But sometimes, like she was looking and thinking about something else. Like she was waiting, and she might as well wait here as somewhere else. She didn't fidget or look restless, waiting with purpose. Her showing up early was the first thing I'd seen her urgent about since it happened. Since I did it.

My story was straight. I had no motive. The DA didn't look a gift horse in the mouth, and I didn't tell him to. He had three cases to wrap up. My affidavits were signed; the rest, he'd said, was a put-on.

The coloureds would tell their version of the story, but Roy's fancy Defense attorneys had nothing on me. I panicked and fell into the bloody mud. I didn't even say he killed her. I said I didn't know, but the police say he did. I only saw what I saw. No further questions.

★

C·P·SERRET/ PLAYING GOD/ XI.

That godforsaken bastard is dead, Sara said when I got into her car in front of the school.

He'd been in a coma for a week. I asked,

—Did he say anything?

—No. The police didn't say when they called, but the papers say he never woke up – I should have checked them this morning.

Sara gave me a refolded newspaper from the back seat. Roy's picture. A lineup of three girls, ending with smiling-braces Izabel. I said,

—It's over, then. What are your parents going to do?

—What can we do? She will never come home, but we will leave her room the way it is. Actually, come back with me today. I'll help you study. Finals week, correct?

—Yes, everyone is stressed out.

She'd never driven Izabel to school or helped her study. Like she was doing too much to make up for it.

It didn't feel real that Roy was dead. That it was over. There'd be no trial. No judgement – or the lynch mob had taken that for themselves. Of course, they didn't call it a lynching. Not up here. Not in 1970. It was college kids rioting in front of a public library. What was another riot? Page 3 behind all of the other news: thirty or more white students, no rope, and no witnesses that would say anything. That's how it was north of the Mason-Dixon.

But someone had riled those boys up and led them to their target, the well-to-do son of a lawyer. Sara said,

—He should never have left his house. Never posted bail and stayed in jail where he belonged. I should have been there when it happened.

I should've been there. I should've seen Roy die too. He'd owed me that much.

Sara chewed her thumb, but she had such clean, neat nails. I'd asked where she'd gone that afternoon after she'd dropped me off at home. She'd said a drive. A long drive. She'd gone for a lot of long drives since Izabel.

Izabel got her own school conference and rainbow bunches of flowers at her locker. Then, she'd been forgotten after the janitor cleared the dried, dead things away.

Mrs K was lying down when we got to her house, and Mr K was home early from work. The perfect family was all awry.

Sara locked her bedroom door from the inside, then sat against the headboard on her bed. I put my rucksack on the floor and took out my notebooks. I sat with them between us, but she didn't look at them. She didn't blink. Her eyes were red. I hadn't noticed in the car.

She was a still life, a painting, till she hit me. I flinched in surprise, not because she'd hit me hard. Then she hit me again. And again.

I didn't feel it on the outside, only in my chest. It was the worst, but my eyes were dry.

—What did you do? she said.

Sara hit me again.

—What... did... you... do?

She pulled a shoebox from under her bed. Izabel's shoebox. Izabel took me out on a date to a new Western, *A Man Called Horse*. She gave me the whole Sunday, and I couldn't believe it – but it was all to bring me back to her room. To show me, to remind me I was her dog.

—No! I said.

Sara hit me again, and I offered the other cheek. I had no defense.

—What did you do to her, Ellie?

The tears were in her voice but not in her eyes either. She threw them at me one at a time: Izabel's Polaroids. The ones she'd taken of me. I couldn't cry, but I was shaking. My atonement, but not Sara, not like this, please.

Izabel had made a trick bottom and kept them under a pair of shoes she didn't like. Not much of a trick if a mother or sister took them out. Mrs K handing the box to Mutti: that's what I'd seen coming.

Mutti knew – all three of them did – but it wasn't something Vati's family or anybody else needed to know, so they kept it quiet. But with these, they'd have to do something. Send me away? It was the bad ending I was ready for.

Now, it was ruined. Ruined.

I looked into those eyes that had always held me, at the lips that said those words. But it wasn't fair if Sara didn't know what I was. If she'd made a mistake and said »I love you« to the wrong one.
—I fucked her, I said, making it ugly. I fucked her like all of the boys who fucked her but not exactly.

Sara hit me again, hard this time, and stars crossed the room sideways. They might have heard it downstairs. The hand that slapped me became a fist.
—How did you make Isa do it? She wasn't like that. She wasn't like you.

She was Isa again now that she was dead. The dead baby of the family.

I picked one up. An image of my eyes, my face obscured, wedged between white thighs: my furrowed brow, my dark crown, but not where my nose was buried. I showed it to Sara.
—This is proof of ownership, I said. My dog collar. I was her broute-gazon. Her dog ¶. See, I said. Nobody really likes it when a dog licks your hand or your face or sticks their nose in your rear, but it worships you. It worships you, and it will eat off the floor for you and wag its tail. There's a song like that, isn't there? I *Wanna Be Your Dog*? Her and her songs…

That's what I'd thought, anyway, till the other girl proved me wrong. I said,
—I don't know what she was ¶. O, see this one. It's just my face, but she said it was her favourite. See, there, on my cheek: it's dripping.

Sara snatched them and tried to tear them but they wouldn't tear and crumpling them tossed them across the room. I took the rubberbanded set from the box.
—And these! Isa dumped me after Hanukkah – you didn't know that, did you? She had the boys giving her all that attention, and I was last year's friend ¶. But she knew about us, Sara. She heard us talking outside; she knew something happened over Thanksgiving – that you'd put a hickie on my neck. So there was one last little thing she wanted me to do for her so she'd be all ready for the boys. So she'd be perfect like she always was ¶. So I did what she wanted. I let her use me, and I believed – I really believed – it was over ¶. Only she

liked it my way, and when she came back to me, I was grateful. I was her last choice, and she didn't want me, and I was grateful 'cause she didn't throw me away! But… but I got mad at her one time because I hated it. Hated that the boys always came first. I said, »Go and touch yourself already! ¶« And she said, sweet as pie, »Go on and show me how.« She took every stitch off of me; she wouldn't let me close my eyes or turn away. I had to look at her, at her and her camera, the flash bulb making my eyes smart ¶. See? You can see everything. I've got no secrets left. Nothing private – you don't need that drawing you showed me back then.

—The other pictures, Sara said. Did you see?

—What other pictures? Was it the other girl? Where are they?

—Another girl? My God, no. The other box was boys, but only… only their *things*. And on each one, she wrote a name. Like trophies. I burned them in the fireplace, but they made a horrible stink. I thought, perhaps, they're not hers. Maybe she got them…

Sara's words failed. It was worse than I'd imagined, but I wasn't surprised that she'd treated them like me. A collection of things. Sara looked like she was being strangled.

—How could this… ? Why didn't you stop her?

—Who's the boss? I said. The girl who kept the pictures, owned the camera, and bought the film with her allowance, or the naked girl? This naked girl ¶? Yes, I knew what she was doing. Why she wanted them. Does that put me in charge? Does Monsieur Pattes get mad when he sees his leash?

I held one photo in front of her face. She closed her eyes.

—Why didn't you come to me?

—You can blame me, Sara. You can hit me. You can blame me for everything if you like. Maybe you'd be right. Every dirty thing she wanted, every dirty thing she heard about somewhere, I did it all. Why? Because I wanted to. Because she let me. She didn't have to force me, really. Well, these… these weren't easy, but,

I swallowed.

—Mostly, I needed her *permission* ¶. After you've put your face back there, where the sun don't shine, you can't see it in the mirror, but you always know; it marks you. I'm guilty.

There's nobody left who's more guilty than I am. So hit me, Sara. Hit me all you want. I'll never ever fight back.

And then, finally, I began to cry. Sara was so far away. And I'd blamed her, was still blaming her, for pushing me away. I'd never escape Izabel, would I? There was a new spear in my side, and I was holding it. And Sara would never escape the lynch mob and the death of a boy she didn't know and the noose I'd put in her hands.

And then Sara's arms were around me, and she held me close, her cheek against my head.

—You can't! I said. I'm dirty! I'm so dirty. It's too late. You should have saved me when I asked. Before she got me...

Sara touched my face, my dirty face. I was so lonely. Izabel made me so alone, and it hurt so much.

—You're wrong, Ellie. Look at me ¶. What was I thinking when I took you to my room at midnight? When I poured vodka in you and showed you those things? And then you fell into my arms, and I... It was *my* mistake ¶. Look at me! I don't know why Isa became that way, but she couldn't have done these evil things if I hadn't...

—No, I said. My mother called your mother. Told her about me. Isa knew, but I guess they never told you ¶. Isa tricked me, too, at the pictures. I kissed her, but that's all she wanted, then. To be ready when she kissed a boy. But one thing led to another thing and another. Nothing you did would've stopped her.

—I could've tried. I could have kept Isa from sneaking out all of those nights. Could have told Maman... Something! Now, they can't know. It will only hurt them with nothing gained. We can leave them the Isa of their memory, but can you?

—I loved her, I said, and it's my secret too.

—These aren't love, Ellie. This isn't what love looks like. You're so messed up; you don't know what love is.

—Don't I? It was a surprise, but I thought, maybe... maybe I was wrong.

—My Ellie, she said. What can I do if I have these feelings for my little sister's friend? One she abused in this way? What can I do? What should I do? I already tried to take advantage – no, I did take advantage. You're not the only one who is guilty.

I heard what she was really saying. What she was trying to say.

—You're going to leave me. You have to.

—No, she said, holding me tighter. I won't abandon you again. I see how you've been abandoned. Such a special girl and so alone.

—But then, we should've been...

—No, Ellie. Love isn't using you that way ¶. I'll take you out sometimes like you asked. Give you some time away from that house. And, if your parents say yes, I'll see if I can take you away, at least for a little while, this summer.

My heart leapt, and I could have kissed her. It would have been as easy as kissing Izabel at the movie house, and remembering, I stopped myself.

—You're not just saying that, right?

—I'll clean this up, and we'll go downstairs. Play something for me on Amadio's piano. They tuned it for Hanukkah, but no one's touched it since then.

—Play what? I haven't started on the next big piece yet, with all this hanging over us.

—Make something up, she said, shrugging.

—I don't know Jazz.

—You know a lot of music; play whatever you want.

—What about Misses K? You said she was lying down.

—I don't think a piano will hurt. Not yours.

Sara gathered the Polaroids back into the shoebox, and it went back under her bed.

—I'll burn this when they're out, and I can open the windows.

She checked on her parents. They were in their room but said it was okay for me to play.

My day of atonement. How had it come to this? I opened the blonde-wood Pleyel.

Sara sat in the corner of the sofa closest to the piano, her legs folded, and lit a cigarette, her Zippo a ringing bell. I was there again, within her eyes.

I was someplace unexpected. What could I see from here? What could I hear? I began with *Barcarolle*, slow, almost at a standstill, then new notes, the old notes I'd heard for a long time. The nameless music I'd failed to find, her gaze wrapped around me, nuzzling my neck from behind.

My heart began to race, and the notes took flight. The future. Was there more to it than chasing the piano from stage to stage, from applause to applause? Was there a home out there for the boarder? Someplace safe and warm. Could I say »I love you«, too? Could I learn the words I'd never heard?

Who was she? What was her music? She'd let me tune the radio however I liked in her car. She, with her walls of books and the big square glasses hidden in her purse. Was it poetry, maybe, on those big shelves?

Who did I know? The Germans and a few things from English class. English, with all its French words, had a different music than High German. I didn't know the French poets, but I had Alkan and Ravel. Would it speak to her if I danced between them? Between *Barcarolle*, *Ondine* and *Emerson*? For a Sephardi with her French and Turkish – and English, American English, the bridge between us? My melody leaping across them, I found a new sonata.

Then *Le Gibet*. We were up there together. The noose for us both. Could I say »I love you« before it was too late? If it wasn't Izabel, could I learn what those words really meant?

I rested my fingers on the keys, and her heart was in her eyes. How had I not seen or understood it? How could I have? You had to know what a heart looked like.

The *no* on her lips wasn't there. Maybe it was a *not yet*. A *someday*. A *one day*. They reflected a question: where was my heart? Could I find it? Could I feel it? Could I show it to her? And what else was in hers?

—Can you show me your books? I said. The ones you like?

Her eyes widened, and she burst into laughter. The most beautiful music I'd ever heard.

★

C·P·SERRET,
PLAYING GOD, XII.

Sara took me to a salon, and I got my hair cut super short. A pixie. I didn't know how warm my neck was till it was cool.

She cut her hair too. Not as short as mine, but it curled up and went wild.

—How do I look? she asked me

—Like Medusa, I said. Beautiful and terrifying.

I was wrong. For Sara, it was the Arab and Persian poets, not the French. I'd never have guessed; I'd never heard of them till she'd read Rumi and Hafiz to me:

A flower-tinted cheek, the flowery close
Of the fair earth, these are enough for me –
Enough that in the meadow wanes and grows
The shadow of a graceful cypress-tree.

She'd had the book open but hadn't looked at the words.

I didn't say it aloud, but were going steady. What else could I call it? We didn't hold hands or anything like that. Nothing that Izabel and I used to do in junior high, but Sara admitted she wasn't »entertaining interest« from anybody else. She said she was too busy, and I didn't poke the hornet's nest. Why spoil a good thing?

She kept reminding me she was twenty like she was reminding herself, and I didn't say anything. I had dinner at her house a lot, or we went out into the City. We saw live Jazz and Blues, and I think I got what Herr Klossner was saying. I wasn't going to play coloured music, but there was more I could do with my repertoire. I'd be ready to make the most of conservatory.

When Sara proposed the trip, Mutti only said, »Two weeks without the piano? Good, go.«

We went up the coast to our first motel. A double-decker marshmallow with a small green pool I didn't like the look of, and from the looks of it, nobody else did either.

She got us a room with double beds. We didn't look like sisters, but that was the story. They didn't say anything.

—What's with the trousers all of a sudden? I said from the second-level rail while she brought up the last bag.
—They're freeing, she said. Kind of swooshy. Don't you like them?
—Guess I'm not that kind of girl. I like my dresses.
—A girly girl. Some are like that.
—What else would I be like?
Sara didn't answer till we were in our room, the door shut.
—There aren't any nice words. Inverts. Dikes. I don't know if you've seen the ones who look like men…
—Like tomboys?
—But grown up. And tomboys still like boys.
—Then what am I? What are we?
—Like I said. There are no nice words. Leslies? Lesbos?
—We're just *us*, then, I said.
—And *we*, she added, smiling.
Sara put her valise on one of the beds. I started unzipping my dress.
—You want to push the beds together, or… ?
She stared at me in my underthings.
—What are you doing?
—Taking off my things.
—Put your dress back on! And no, we're not pushing the beds together. That's not why we're here.
—But I want to with you, I said, stepping out of it and leaving it on the floor. And I haven't in so long.
—Ellie! Put it back on, or we're checking out. I'll take you straight home!
—Fine! I said, snatching it up. You've seen everything; why're you being such a square?
—Don't test me, Ellie, I'm not made of stone. I quit pot and drinking for a reason.
—What, for me?
—Who else, Ellie?
—You never said.
Her voice was soft.
—After what happened, did I have to spell it out?
—But it's not like that now. I want to make love with you. Don't you want to?

I'd never said that before. Those words: »Make love«. Like in the pictures.

Sara stopped unpacking her things and sat across from me on the edge of her bed, her hands in her lap.

—I should take you home after telling you this, but...

—Then, don't... !

—You must know, she insisted, not raising her voice. Now that I have you here, like this. I am not a... an angel, Ellie. I was a senior in high school when you and Isa became friends. The first time I saw you, remember ¶? I didn't understand why you stood out to me, then, like a light shone on you. Yes, you were sweet and charming and talented, like Isa, though you didn't try so hard to be winning as she did. But there was something else, Ellie, a recognition.

She touched her chest.

—I felt it here when you looked at me. Like something was waiting, and you were the spark, but once the flame was lit, it was lit forever. And you were so young and my baby sister's friend. And I flirted with you, prensesim. And I think you were afraid, and you were right to be. Because it was wrong of me, even if we are the same, as if I were a man trying to seduce a young girl.

Her atonement. Why she'd bent her life into a pretzel to pick me up before and after school every day. My piano lessons. »It's not safe« made sense, maybe, for a week or two till the hubbub settled down. Here was the real reason, and my weak knees dropped me back onto my bed.

—I was jealous of Isa, Sara was saying, and became very mean to her. I can see that now; it ate at me. When I pushed you away, it was for the right reasons, but I did it the wrong way. You had no one to turn to. I didn't know you were so alone and that Isa was what she was. What she did was monstrous ¶. I'm afraid I'll let myself consume you. Take you away from the future you should have, to keep you for myself. I want you to grow and become who you should be. I adore your passion, the way you laugh and smile. I want to meet you again as adult Ellie, when you've caught up. When you have your own place in the world.

It was so clear. I said it to hear it:

—Isa didn't love me at all.

I hadn't really felt it till then, despite everything Izabel did. I was so blind.

—I was so blind, I said aloud. She wanted... she made me promise to give up conservatory.

—How awful, why?

—So that I could go to music school at whatever college she went to. So that I'd be right there whenever she wanted me.

—Ah, you haven't told me everything.

—No. You know, mostly, just not all of the particulars.

—I'm sorry, chérie, but I think I need to know.

It took a long time, but I told her everything but one thing, and at the end, she broke down. I wanted to go to her, but it wouldn't be fair. There was no way she couldn't see it now. Nobody had more motive than me.

I hadn't gotten away with it. My atonement was only delayed. I heard it again: *Le Gibet*. Did I have any last words? Yes.

—There was going to be another Shoah, I said. It's been averted, and whatever happened to me, maybe it had to. I don't know. But Roy, the people who were starting to follow him... History was going to repeat itself.

—Can you be certain? she said through the tears. He had a family too.

—You can't be born without one. Are you sad for them, or were they responsible for him?

—I was responsible for Isa. We all were. Me. Maman, Papa. How did we let her become this? She was a monster.

Izabel never loved me, but she came out into the rain when I told her not to. Why would she be worried about me? I wouldn't cry. I wouldn't.

I'd killed her with my own hands, and Sara had killed Roy with others'. She'd shown me what it was to be loved, and if that was over now, it was fair. She'd saved the world, not me. I was afraid his evil would have spread from prison. I'd never tell, never hint what she'd done, not even on the gibbet, right till the end.

Sara said she needed to wash up and took some things with her into the shower, but I could hear her crying again. I got dressed and, taking my sun hat, went out by the repulsive pool. There were lounge chairs but no shade, and the sun was hotter than I liked. I had no piano, my fingers drumming out *Scarbo* under the spotlight, trapped in my final time with Izabel, her on top, grinding against me, her hand over my mouth.

There was no more talk of going back, but Sara was quiet for a few days. She seemed to find herself again as we went north from motel to motel along the seaboard, renewed maybe, as she tanned a light gold, like the Persian girl I'd thought Izabel might be once upon a time.

At a rocky beach where people couldn't swim, we saw the last fisherman packing his things into his wagon when we got there. Sara let me link my arm with hers or hold her hand like it'd been so long ago with Izabel, but different. In my heart and mind, *Barcarolle*, but that was just me.

—You're so brown, Sara said; it's like magic.

She ran one hand down my arm, then jerked back like she'd done wrong.

—You don't have to stop, I said. My answer to you is always *yes*.

She laughed but tried to frown at me, one hand on her hip.

—Ellie, never say that to anyone.

—Even you?

—Even me. Your *no* is very important. You belong to yourself. No matter who you're with, you can always say *no*.

I was dazzled again, golden light filling my eyes like I could see her soul. The sun could never be so bright.

—I love you, Sara. I said. O, Sara! I love you.

She held me to her like I was precious – like we were one in this feeling together. The sparkling, spicy scent of her filled me and I kissed her shoulder and she pulled away a little and I tried to kiss her and she shook her head looking at my face.

—Nobody's going to know, I said. The seagulls don't care!

—My Ellie, if I let myself, she said. I'll lose myself. It's not time, not yet. I think I can see who you'll become, and it's wonderful. You have to let flowers bloom.

It's not like I didn't know what she meant. Towards the end, with Izabel, it was like I was sinking, drowning in dark water, and I'd never see the sky again.

They'd known something was happening in my room. I couldn't keep quiet like Izabel did, and she'd laugh at me afterwards. Mutti offered me cigarettes when I'd come down to dinner or when I got back from walking Izabel home. So German, saying I *know* without saying it to the boarder. She didn't offer me after-dinner schnapps, though she'd been drinking more of it without the meal than before.

All the way back in March, I'd asked Izabel if she was afraid Mutti would call her mother. She'd said, »Why would she spoil it? Did you see how she was gloating when we came in ¶? You ruining someone else's daughter after she warned them, and they didn't listen? What's better than that? It's no wonder she hasn't said a word to stop us. She's lovin' every minute out of spite ¶. And besides, who's Maman gonna believe, me or her? She's seen the nice boys walk me home and escort me to the movies. Perfect gentlemen. It's all in your alibi, baby. Gotta keep it airtight. If you've got that, they won't believe their own eyes.«

But Sara and I needed no alibi. Mutti thought the worst of me no matter what.

I waited till bedtime to try again. Sara told me to put on cold cream after all that sun and next time use the Coppertone suntan lotion, but I said I'd be alright, waiting for my chance. I didn't wait till she'd fallen asleep but till her breathing relaxed with the lights off.

—Wake up! I said and planted one on her.

—My God, Ellie, don't you listen? She pushed me back, saying, —We're not going to. No kissing.

—Sara, please, I said. I won't even get under the blanket.

—No, it's not happening tonight.

She sat up and turned the lamp on. I said,

—Then, when?

—Ellie. I wanted to take you from the City and your family, from all of it, not for me but for you. You need to see past all that. Like your tutor said, there's a heaven above the mountains and God too. I'm showing you a little of how big the world is. You aren't trapped in that life, in their world.

—Sara, I said.

—Yes, my Ellie.

—When?

—Crazy girl, get your grown woman's body off me and go back to bed.

Sara reached for the lamp, but I caught her hand and held her eyes.

—When.

She squirmed, but I held firm.

—Ah, I don't know… When… when you're old enough to buy your own drink.

—What? I'll be in conservatory… I'll be almost done!

—So?

—It's too long. I can drink when I'm eighteen; that's more than long enough.

—Twenty-one.

—Eighteen.

—Fine, twenty: my age now.

—Nineteen. Nineteen and not a day longer. On my birthday.

—You're something else.

I went back to my bed. I was beside Sara, where she wanted me to be – where she'd always wanted me to be. Something I'd never have believed back then, but I wanted to be closer. Prensesim. Chérie. She'd always meant it. I reached my hand out to her in the closing dark, a gap between us.

She wasn't ready to see that I didn't have a little kid left in me. She needed those years to let me grow in her eyes; she had to see for herself. But it wouldn't take four years or three-and-a-half. I'd convince her before then.

I wasn't going to give up that easily. In showing me »the world«, she'd put the spotlight on what I wanted for me. I could see it: the dermatologist and the concert pianist. But I wouldn't say anything yet. A maze of flowers would grow up around her, and she wouldn't get away. She won't want to.

It was passing by, that big world, the wind roaring around us with the top down, *Breakfast at Tiffany's* sunglasses 'cause I'd never escape Audrey Hepburn either. Not that Sara said it in so many words, but she'd picked them out. I turned in my seat and watched her drive. She said,

—Don't even think of it.

—What? I'm not touching you.

—I can hear you thinking it from here, and I can't keep up with your dirty mind.

—I'll think about it all I want till my nineteenth birthday.
Sara laughed, finally. She tried too hard to be mature; she didn't make it easy. I lit a cigarette for her and then one for me. Her long white cigarettes, a gold-edged cream box. Virginia Slims. She said,
—Do you want to get milkshakes? There's a Dairy Queen up ahead.
—Yes, I love you. Let's get ice cream.
—Prensesim benim, she said after laughing, but that's not a toy to play with.
—I think it is, I said.
I couldn't stop smiling.
We weren't so far apart. Twenty and fifteen till I turned sixteen in November. Would it be that different at twenty-three and nineteen – she in medical school, me in conservatory? We'd be in different places, for sure, like she was setting up a hurdle in advance till I was done with school. She thought she was so smart. I could see it coming a mile away.

www.ingramcontent.com/pod-product-compliance
Lightning Source LLC
LaVergne TN
LVHW090606110826
845146LV00001B/283

* 9 7 9 8 9 9 2 6 7 0 8 6 8 *